FOND DU LAC PUBLIC LIBRARY

KRYPTO
The SUPERDOG

SUPERMAN CREATED BY
JERRY SIEGEL AND JOE SHUSTER
BY SPECIAL ARRANGEMENT WITH
THE JERRY SIEGEL FAMILY

STONE ARCH BOOKS
a capstone imprint

STONE ARCH BOOKS™
Published in 2014
A Capstone Imprint
1710 Roe Crest Drive
North Mankato, MN 56003
www.capstonepub.com

Originally published by DC Comics in the U.S. in single magazine form as

DC Comics
1700 Broadway, New York, NY 10019
A Warner Bros. Entertainment Company

Cataloging-in-Publication Data is available at the
Library of Congress website
ISBN: 978-1-4342-4785-8 (library binding)

Summary: As the Last Pup of Krypton arrives on Earth, he meets his host family and new friend Kevin, and fights crime! Krypto finds his way to Earth and is adopted by Kevin, his new best friend.

STONE ARCH BOOKS
Ashley C. Andersen Zantop Publisher
Michael Dahl Editorial Director
Donald Lemke & Sean Tulien Editors
Bob Lentz Art Director
Hilary Wacholz Designer

DC COMICS
Kristy Quinn Original U.S. Editor

Printed in China by Nordica.
1013 / CA21301918
092013 007744NORDS14

KRYPTO

THE SUPERDOG ™

Here Comes Krypto

JESSE LEON MCCANN......................................WRITER

MIN. S. KU...PENCILLER

JEFF ALBRECHT...INKER

DAVE TANGUAY...COLORIST

DAVE TANGUAY..LETTERER

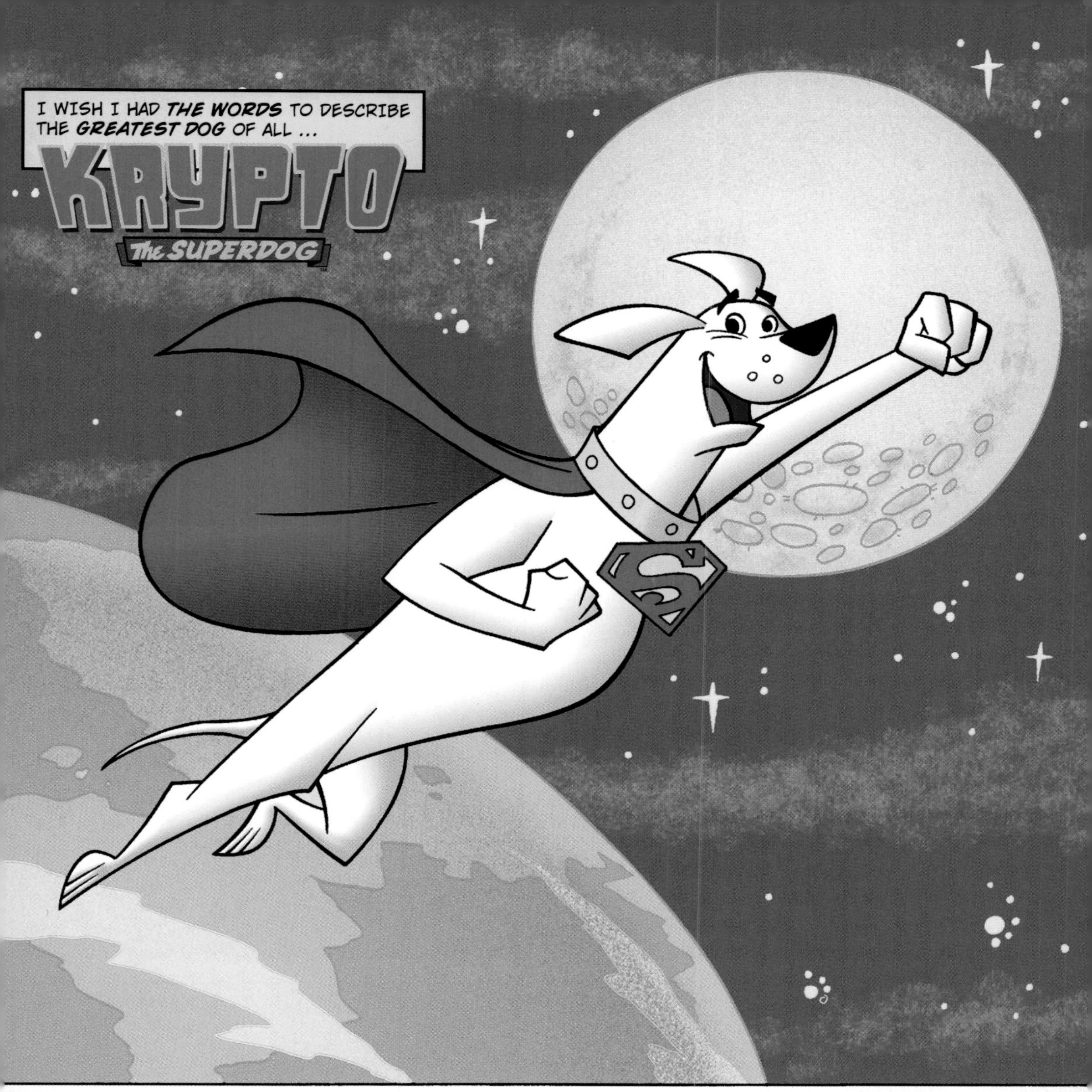
I WISH I HAD THE WORDS TO DESCRIBE THE GREATEST DOG OF ALL ...
KRYPTO
The SUPERDOG

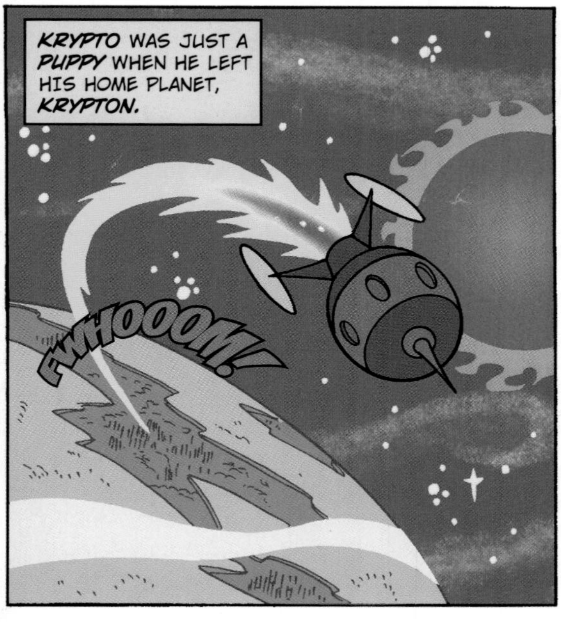
KRYPTO WAS JUST A PUPPY WHEN HE LEFT HIS HOME PLANET, KRYPTON.
FWHOOOM!

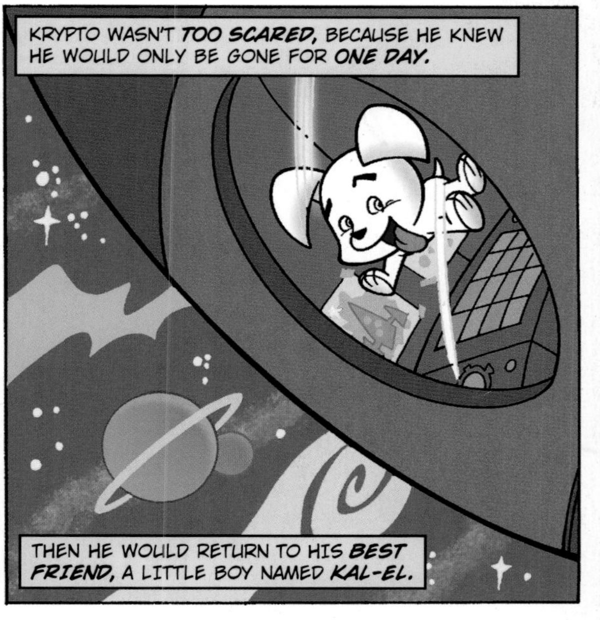
KRYPTO WASN'T TOO SCARED, BECAUSE HE KNEW HE WOULD ONLY BE GONE FOR ONE DAY.
THEN HE WOULD RETURN TO HIS BEST FRIEND, A LITTLE BOY NAMED KAL-EL.

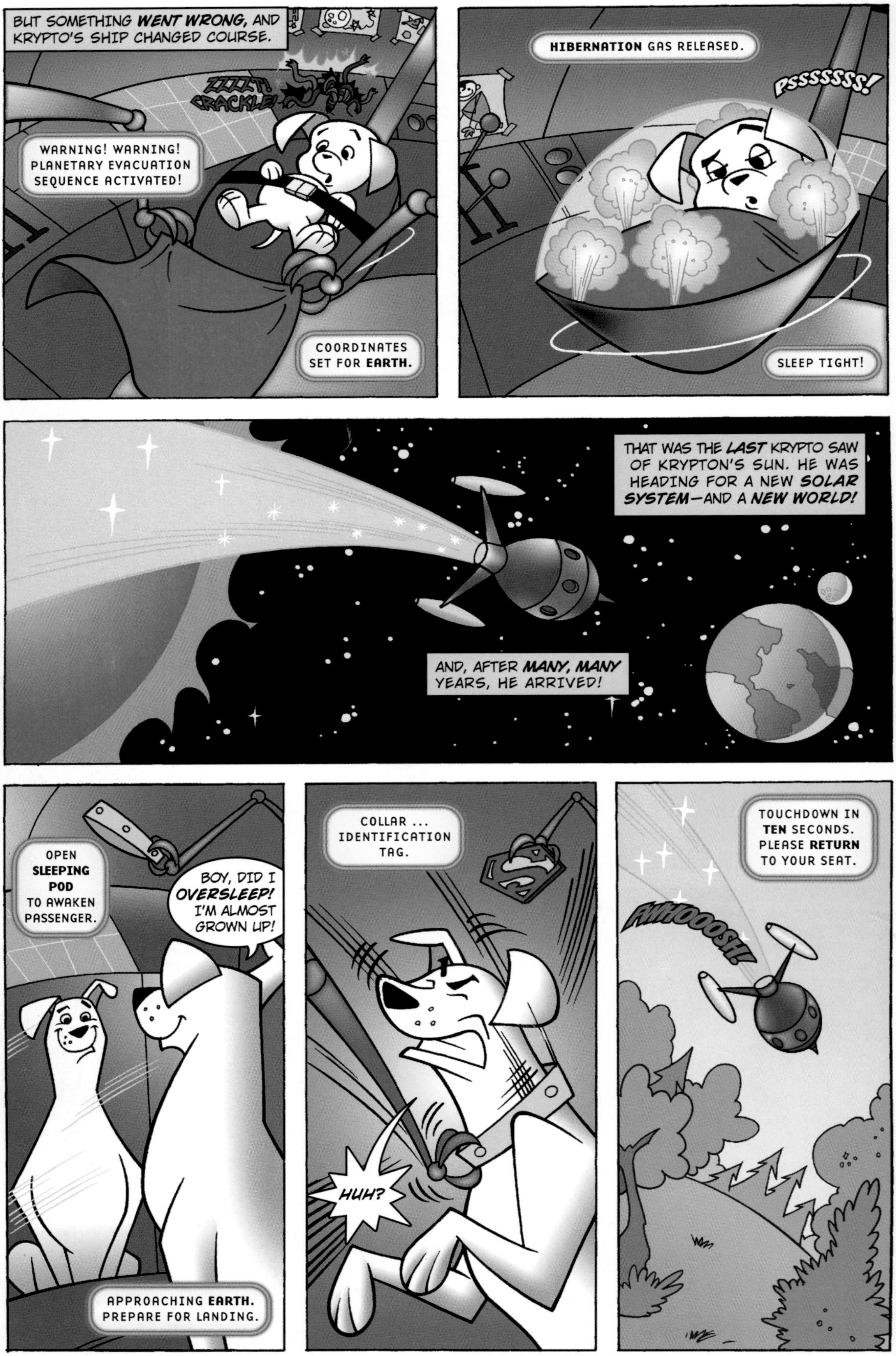

BUT SOMETHING WENT WRONG, AND KRYPTO'S SHIP CHANGED COURSE.
ZZZZT! CRACKLE!
WARNING! WARNING! PLANETARY EVACUATION SEQUENCE ACTIVATED!
COORDINATES SET FOR EARTH.
HIBERNATION GAS RELEASED.
PSSSSSSS!
SLEEP TIGHT!
THAT WAS THE LAST KRYPTO SAW OF KRYPTON'S SUN. HE WAS HEADING FOR A NEW SOLAR SYSTEM—AND A NEW WORLD!
AND, AFTER MANY, MANY YEARS, HE ARRIVED!
OPEN SLEEPING POD TO AWAKEN PASSENGER.
BOY, DID I OVERSLEEP! I'M ALMOST GROWN UP!
APPROACHING EARTH. PREPARE FOR LANDING.
COLLAR ... IDENTIFICATION TAG.
HUH?
TOUCHDOWN IN TEN SECONDS. PLEASE RETURN TO YOUR SEAT.
FWHOOOOSH!

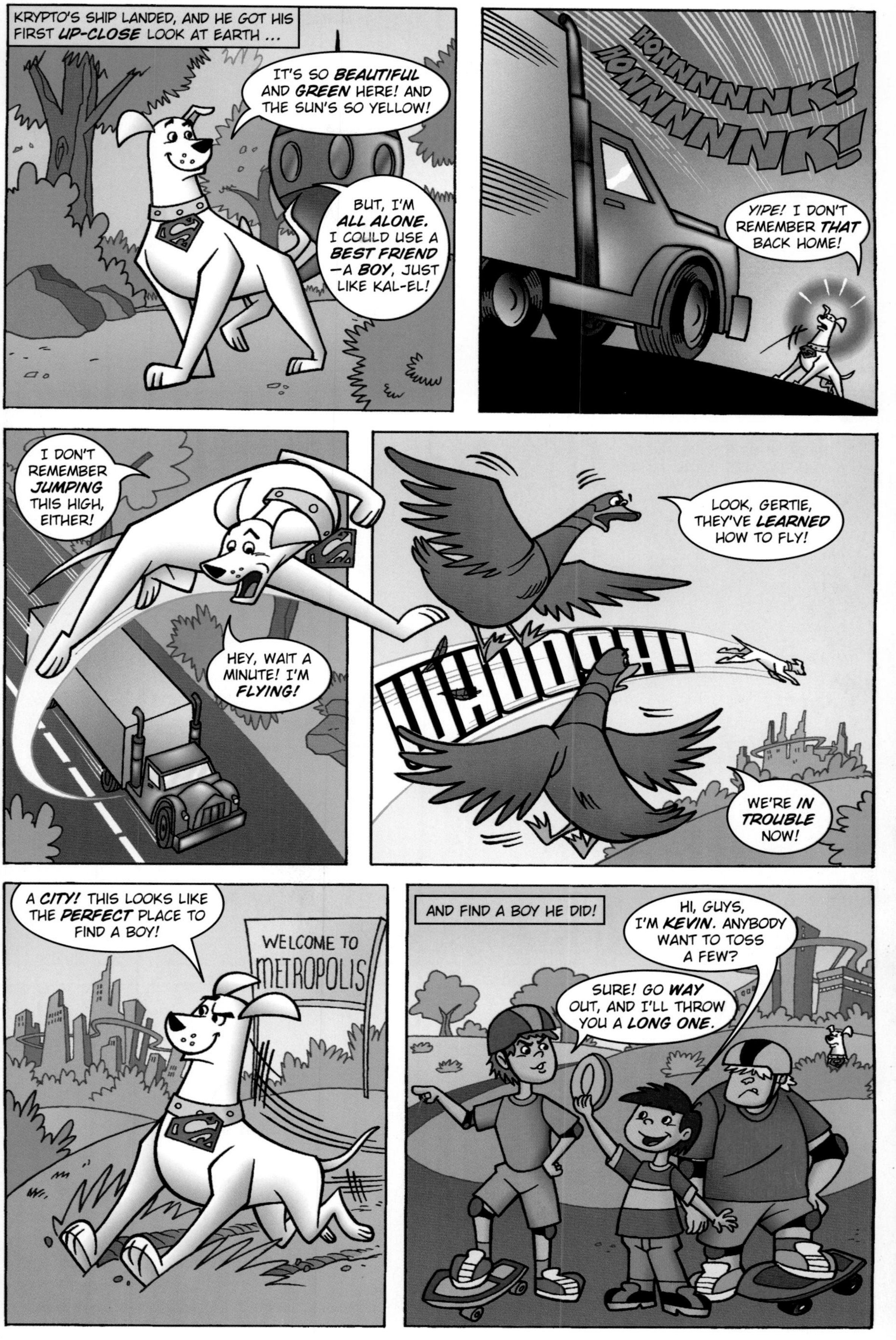
KRYPTO'S SHIP LANDED, AND HE GOT HIS FIRST UP-CLOSE LOOK AT EARTH ...
IT'S SO BEAUTIFUL AND GREEN HERE! AND THE SUN'S SO YELLOW!
BUT, I'M ALL ALONE. I COULD USE A BEST FRIEND —A BOY, JUST LIKE KAL-EL!
HONNNNNK!
HONNNNNNK!
YIPE! I DON'T REMEMBER THAT BACK HOME!
I DON'T REMEMBER JUMPING THIS HIGH, EITHER!
HEY, WAIT A MINUTE! I'M FLYING!
LOOK, GERTIE, THEY'VE LEARNED HOW TO FLY!
WE'RE IN TROUBLE NOW!
A CITY! THIS LOOKS LIKE THE PERFECT PLACE TO FIND A BOY!
WELCOME TO METROPOLIS
AND FIND A BOY HE DID!
HI, GUYS, I'M KEVIN. ANYBODY WANT TO TOSS A FEW?
SURE! GO WAY OUT, AND I'LL THROW YOU A LONG ONE.

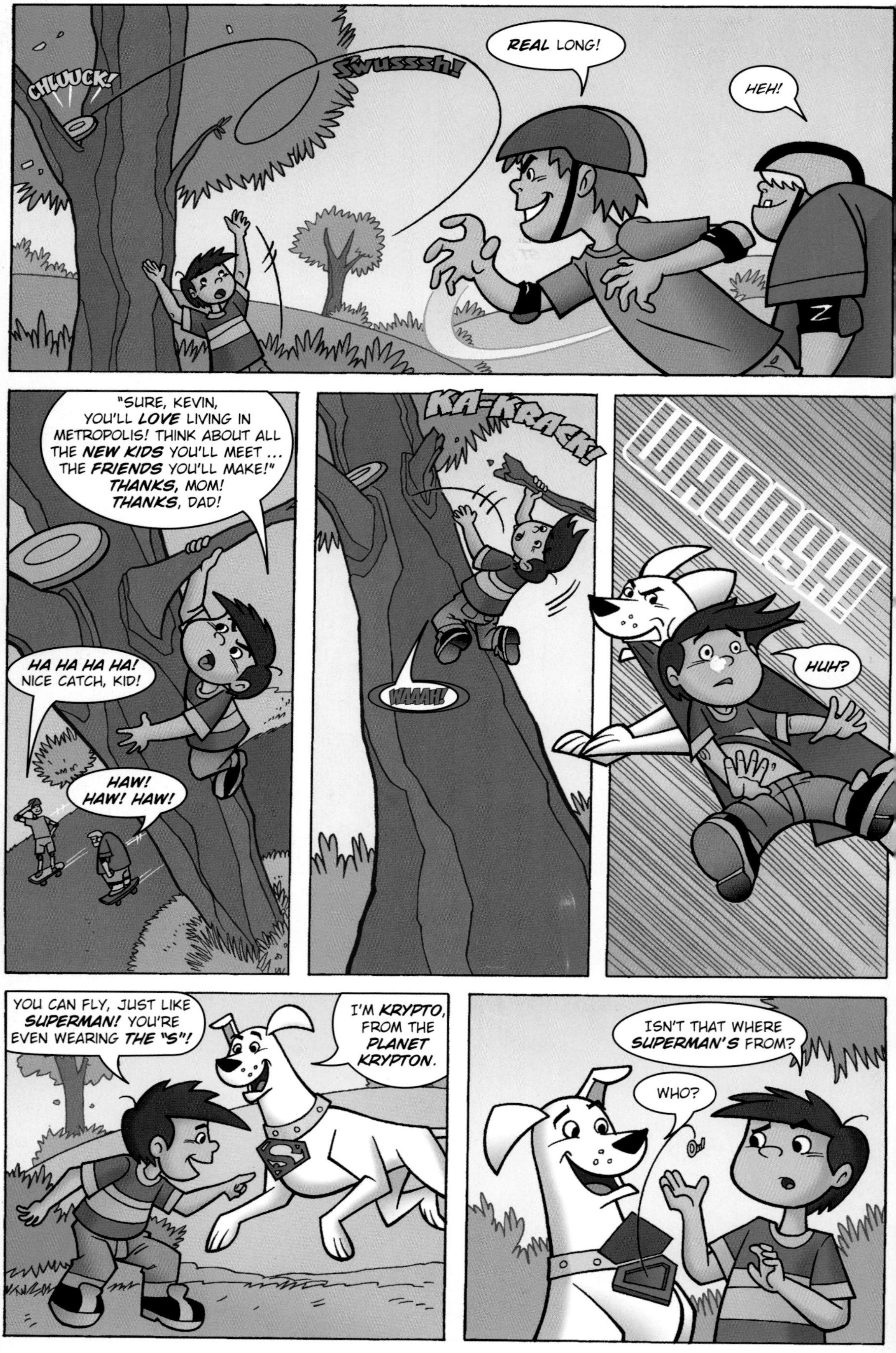
CHLUUCK!
SWUSSSH!
REAL LONG!
HEH!
"SURE, KEVIN, YOU'LL LOVE LIVING IN METROPOLIS! THINK ABOUT ALL THE NEW KIDS YOU'LL MEET ... THE FRIENDS YOU'LL MAKE!" THANKS, MOM! THANKS, DAD!
HA HA HA HA! NICE CATCH, KID!
HAW! HAW! HAW!
KA-KRACK!
WAAAH!
WHOOSH!
HUH?
YOU CAN FLY, JUST LIKE SUPERMAN! YOU'RE EVEN WEARING THE "S"!
I'M KRYPTO, FROM THE PLANET KRYPTON.
ISN'T THAT WHERE SUPERMAN'S FROM?
WHO?

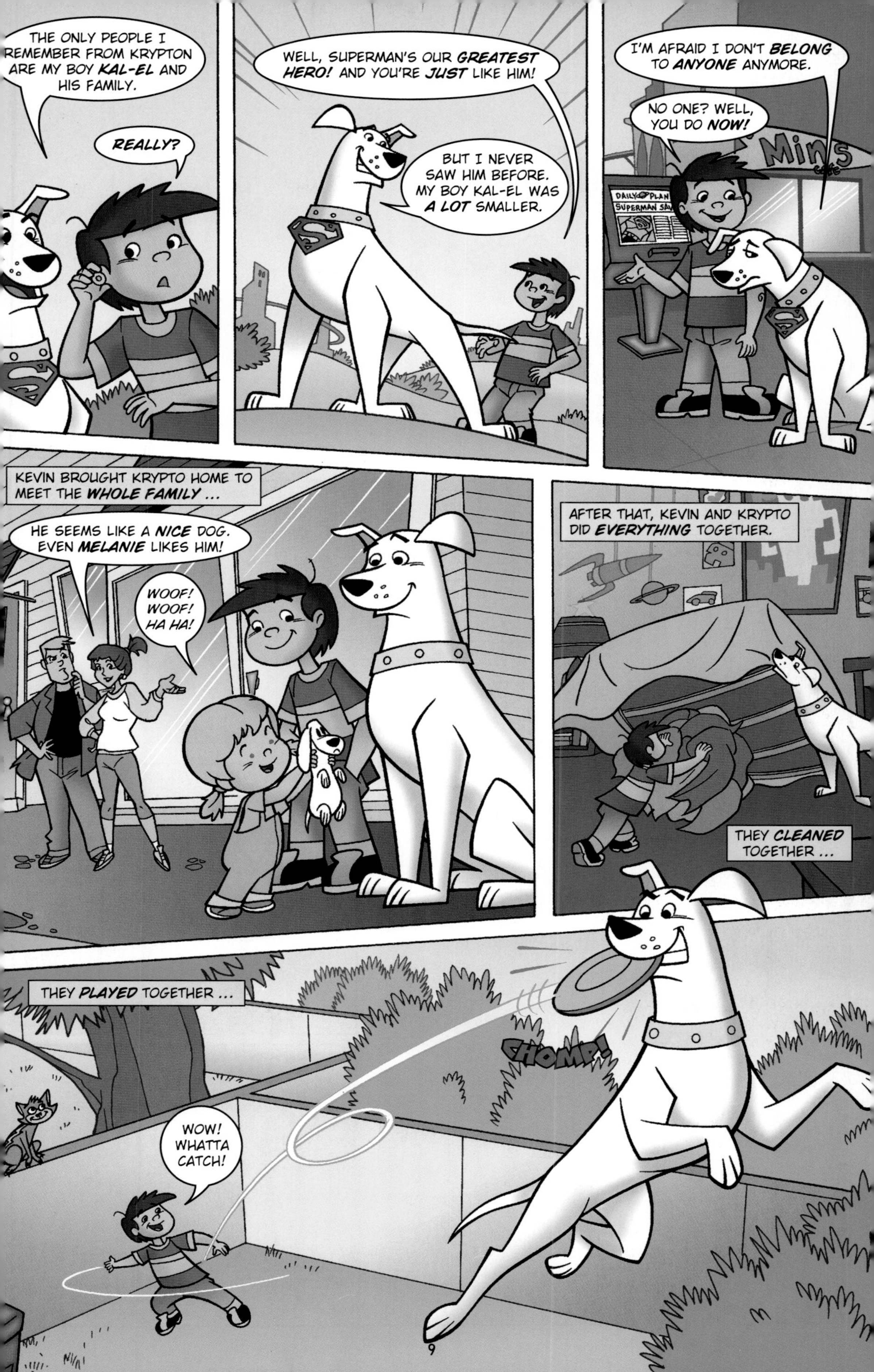
THE ONLY PEOPLE I REMEMBER FROM KRYPTON ARE MY BOY KAL-EL AND HIS FAMILY.
REALLY?
WELL, SUPERMAN'S OUR GREATEST HERO! AND YOU'RE JUST LIKE HIM!
BUT I NEVER SAW HIM BEFORE. MY BOY KAL-EL WAS A LOT SMALLER.
I'M AFRAID I DON'T BELONG TO ANYONE ANYMORE.
NO ONE? WELL, YOU DO NOW!
KEVIN BROUGHT KRYPTO HOME TO MEET THE WHOLE FAMILY ...
HE SEEMS LIKE A NICE DOG. EVEN MELANIE LIKES HIM!
WOOF! WOOF! HA HA!
AFTER THAT, KEVIN AND KRYPTO DID EVERYTHING TOGETHER.
THEY CLEANED TOGETHER ...
THEY PLAYED TOGETHER ...
CHOMP!
WOW! WHATTA CATCH!

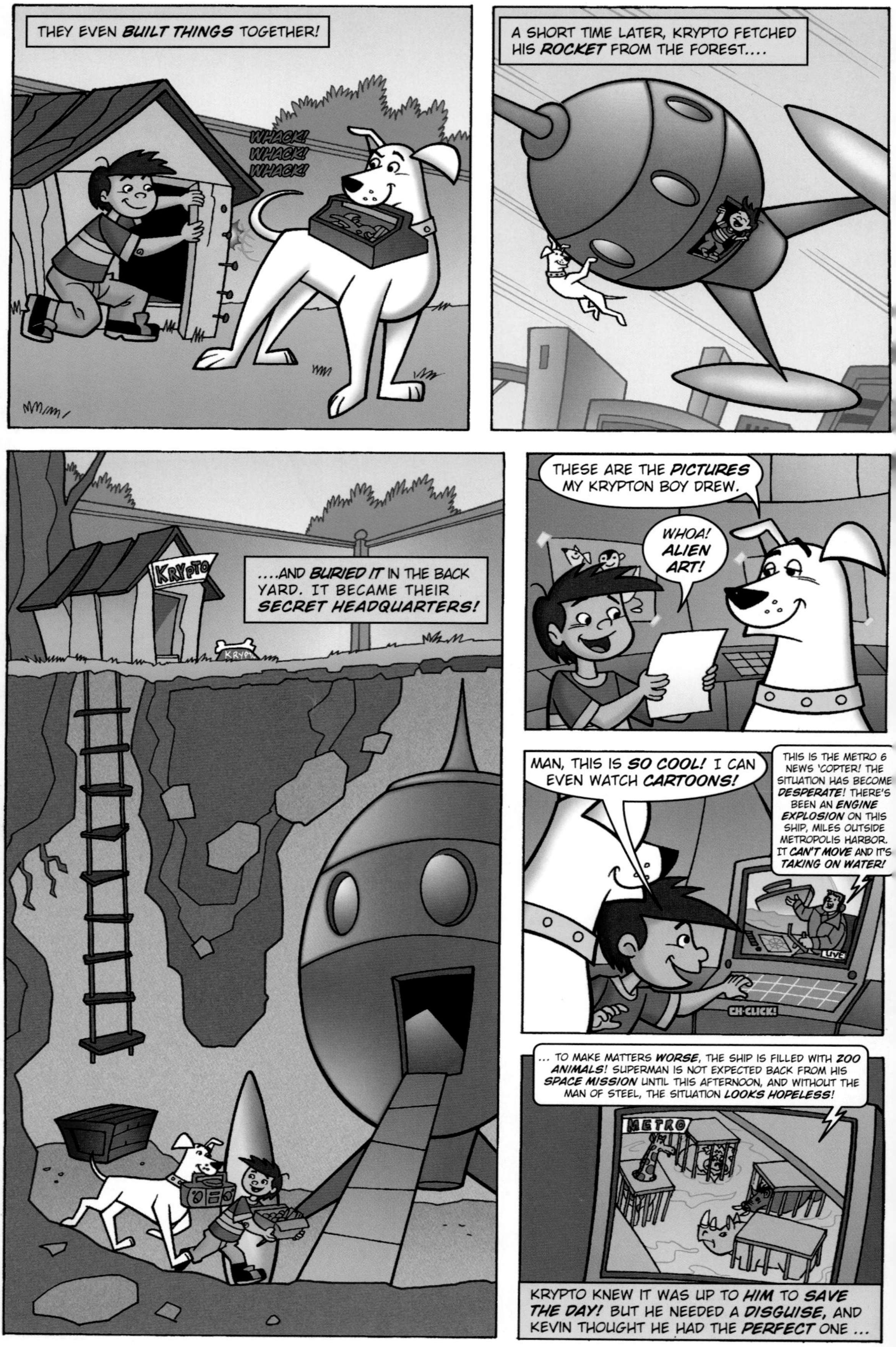
THEY EVEN BUILT THINGS TOGETHER!
WHACK! WHACK! WHACK!
A SHORT TIME LATER, KRYPTO FETCHED HIS ROCKET FROM THE FOREST....
....AND BURIED IT IN THE BACK YARD. IT BECAME THEIR SECRET HEADQUARTERS!
KRYPTO
THESE ARE THE PICTURES MY KRYPTON BOY DREW.
WHOA! ALIEN ART!
MAN, THIS IS SO COOL! I CAN EVEN WATCH CARTOONS!
THIS IS THE METRO 6 NEWS 'COPTER! THE SITUATION HAS BECOME DESPERATE! THERE'S BEEN AN ENGINE EXPLOSION ON THIS SHIP, MILES OUTSIDE METROPOLIS HARBOR. IT CAN'T MOVE AND IT'S TAKING ON WATER!
LIVE
CH-CLICK!
... TO MAKE MATTERS WORSE, THE SHIP IS FILLED WITH ZOO ANIMALS! SUPERMAN IS NOT EXPECTED BACK FROM HIS SPACE MISSION UNTIL THIS AFTERNOON, AND WITHOUT THE MAN OF STEEL, THE SITUATION LOOKS HOPELESS!
METRO
KRYPTO KNEW IT WAS UP TO HIM TO SAVE THE DAY! BUT HE NEEDED A DISGUISE, AND KEVIN THOUGHT HE HAD THE PERFECT ONE ...

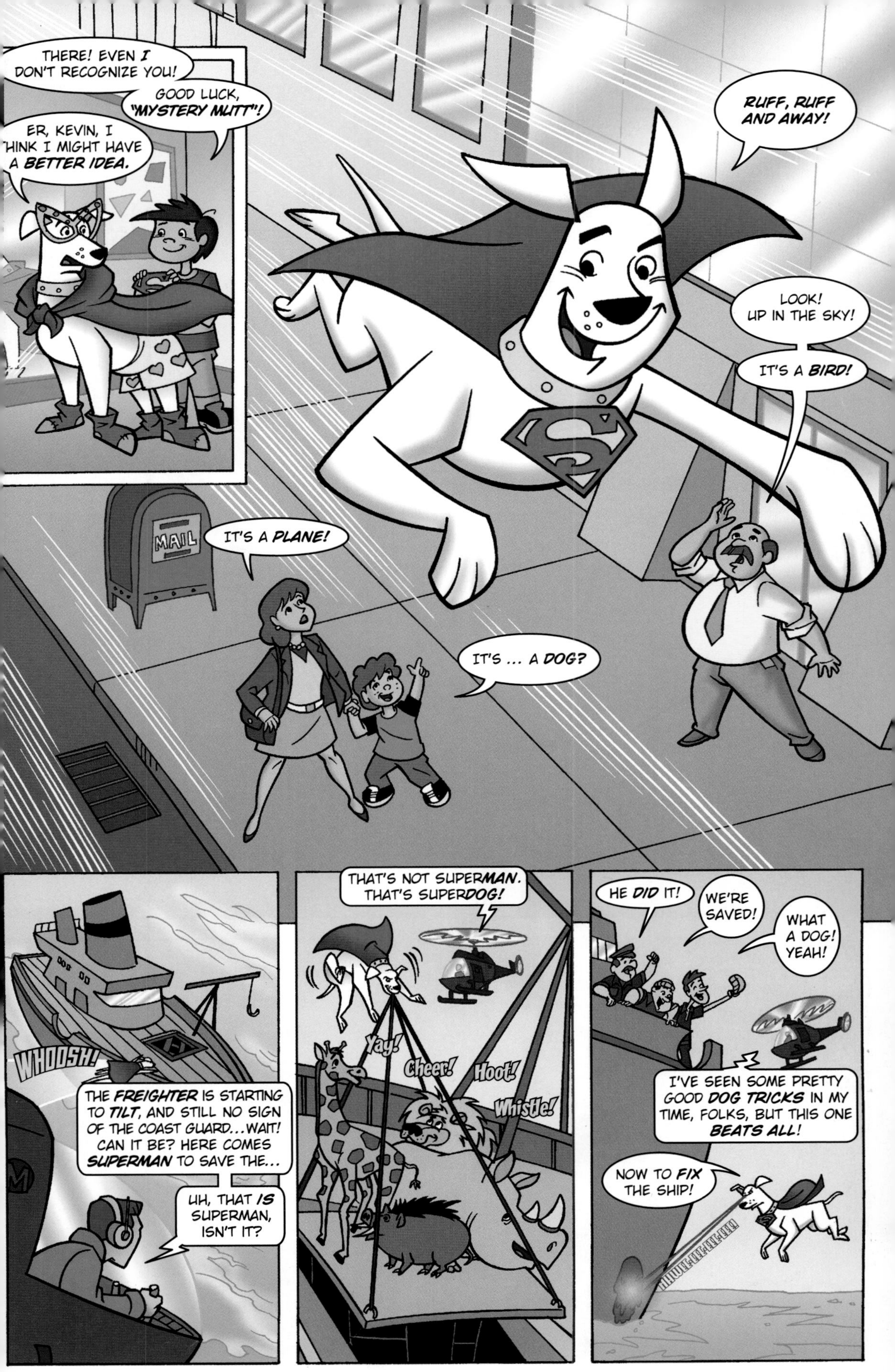
THERE! EVEN I DON'T RECOGNIZE YOU!
GOOD LUCK, "MYSTERY MUTT"!
ER, KEVIN, I THINK I MIGHT HAVE A BETTER IDEA.
RUFF, RUFF AND AWAY!
LOOK! UP IN THE SKY!
IT'S A BIRD!
MAIL
IT'S A PLANE!
IT'S ... A DOG?
WHOOSH!
THE FREIGHTER IS STARTING TO TILT, AND STILL NO SIGN OF THE COAST GUARD... WAIT! CAN IT BE? HERE COMES SUPERMAN TO SAVE THE...
UH, THAT IS SUPERMAN, ISN'T IT?
THAT'S NOT SUPERMAN. THAT'S SUPERDOG!
Yay!
Cheer!
Hoot!
Whistle!
HE DID IT!
WE'RE SAVED!
WHAT A DOG! YEAH!
I'VE SEEN SOME PRETTY GOOD DOG TRICKS IN MY TIME, FOLKS, BUT THIS ONE BEATS ALL!
NOW TO FIX THE SHIP!

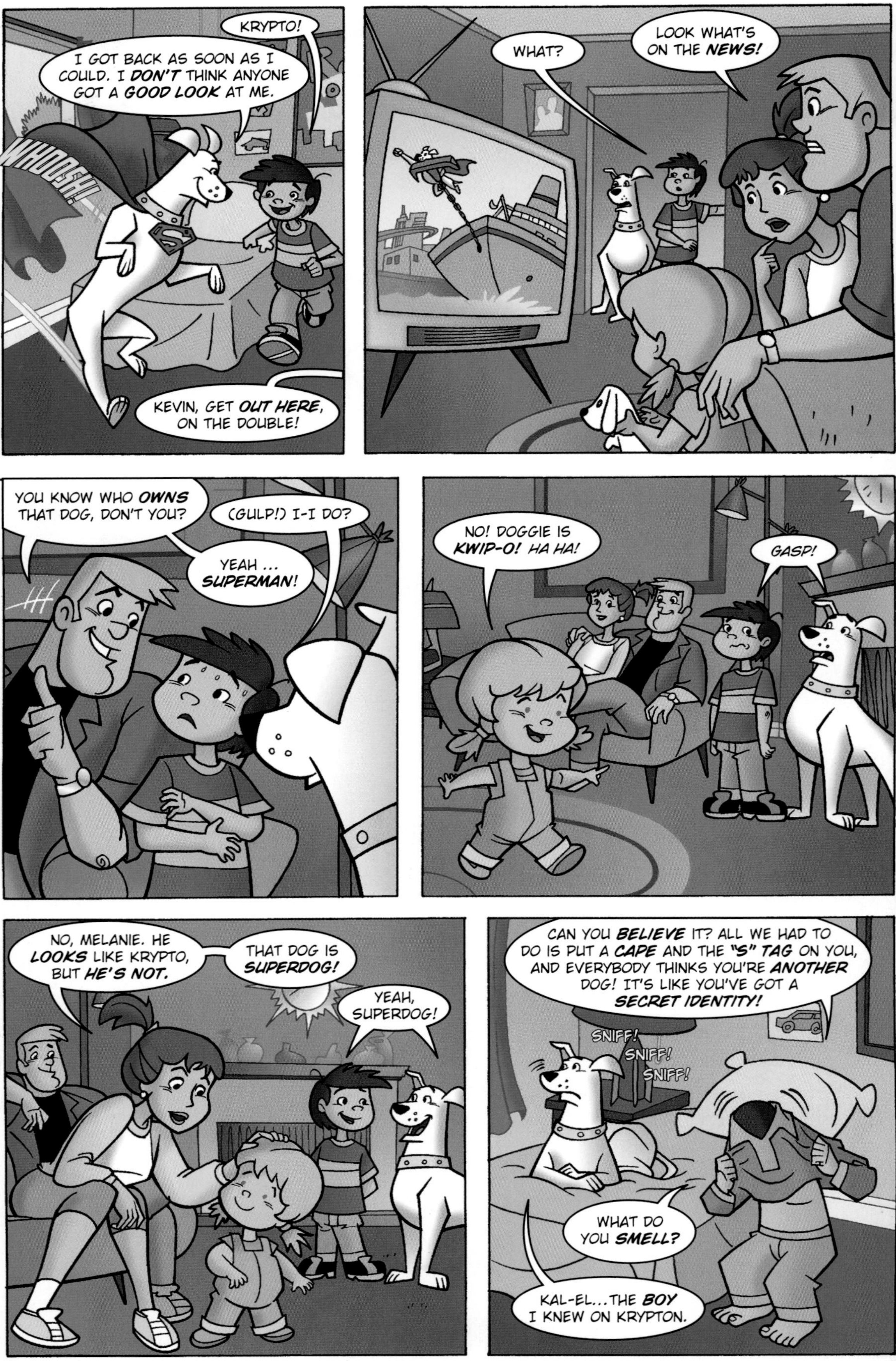

KRYPTO!
I GOT BACK AS SOON AS I COULD. I DON'T THINK ANYONE GOT A GOOD LOOK AT ME.
WHOOSH!
KEVIN, GET OUT HERE, ON THE DOUBLE!
WHAT?
LOOK WHAT'S ON THE NEWS!
YOU KNOW WHO OWNS THAT DOG, DON'T YOU?
(GULP!) I-I DO?
YEAH ... SUPERMAN!
NO! DOGGIE IS KWIP-O! HA HA!
GASP!
NO, MELANIE. HE LOOKS LIKE KRYPTO, BUT HE'S NOT.
THAT DOG IS SUPERDOG!
YEAH, SUPERDOG!
CAN YOU BELIEVE IT? ALL WE HAD TO DO IS PUT A CAPE AND THE "S" TAG ON YOU, AND EVERYBODY THINKS YOU'RE ANOTHER DOG! IT'S LIKE YOU'VE GOT A SECRET IDENTITY!
SNIFF! SNIFF! SNIFF!
WHAT DO YOU SMELL?
KAL-EL...THE BOY I KNEW ON KRYPTON.

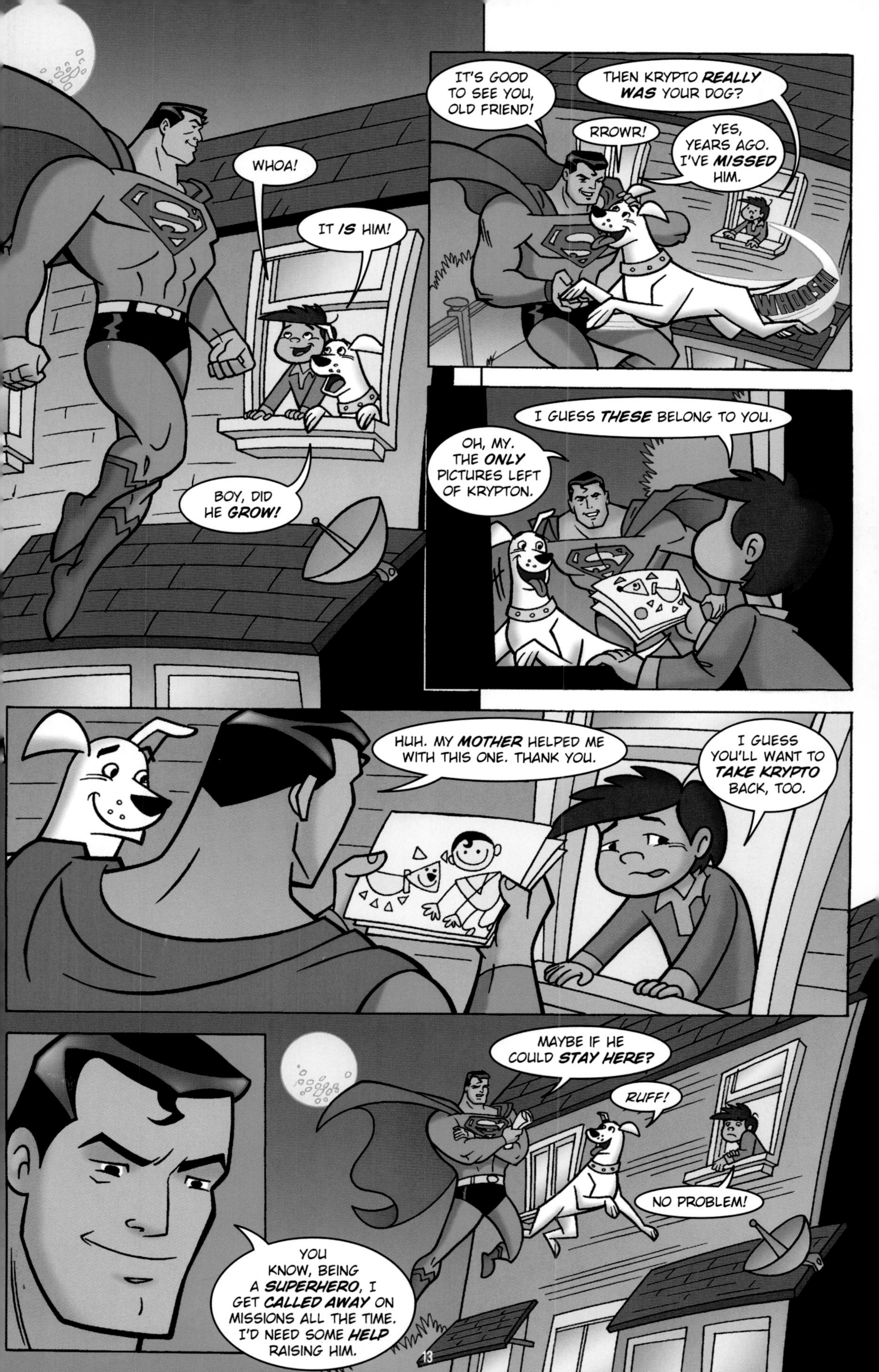
WHOA!
IT IS HIM!
BOY, DID HE GROW!
IT'S GOOD TO SEE YOU, OLD FRIEND!
RROWR!
THEN KRYPTO REALLY WAS YOUR DOG?
YES, YEARS AGO. I'VE MISSED HIM.
WHOOSH!
I GUESS THESE BELONG TO YOU.
OH, MY. THE ONLY PICTURES LEFT OF KRYPTON.
HUH. MY MOTHER HELPED ME WITH THIS ONE. THANK YOU.
I GUESS YOU'LL WANT TO TAKE KRYPTO BACK, TOO.
YOU KNOW, BEING A SUPERHERO, I GET CALLED AWAY ON MISSIONS ALL THE TIME. I'D NEED SOME HELP RAISING HIM.
MAYBE IF HE COULD STAY HERE?
RUFF!
NO PROBLEM!

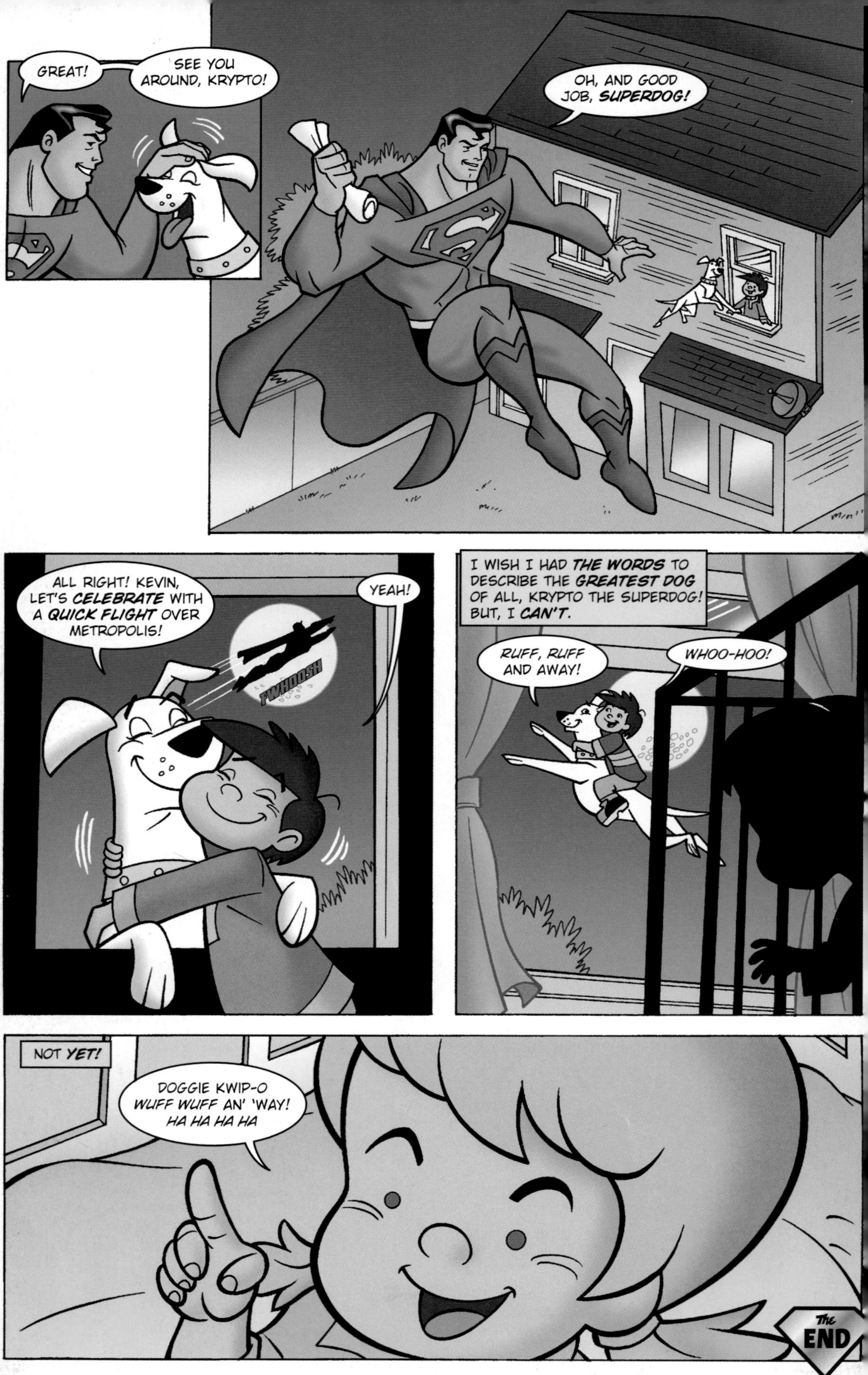
GREAT!
SEE YOU AROUND, KRYPTO!
OH, AND GOOD JOB, SUPERDOG!
ALL RIGHT! KEVIN, LET'S CELEBRATE WITH A QUICK FLIGHT OVER METROPOLIS!
YEAH!
FWHOOSH
I WISH I HAD THE WORDS TO DESCRIBE THE GREATEST DOG OF ALL, KRYPTO THE SUPERDOG! BUT, I CAN'T.
RUFF, RUFF AND AWAY!
WHOO-HOO!
NOT YET!
DOGGIE KWIP-O WUFF WUFF AN' 'WAY! HA HA HA HA
The END

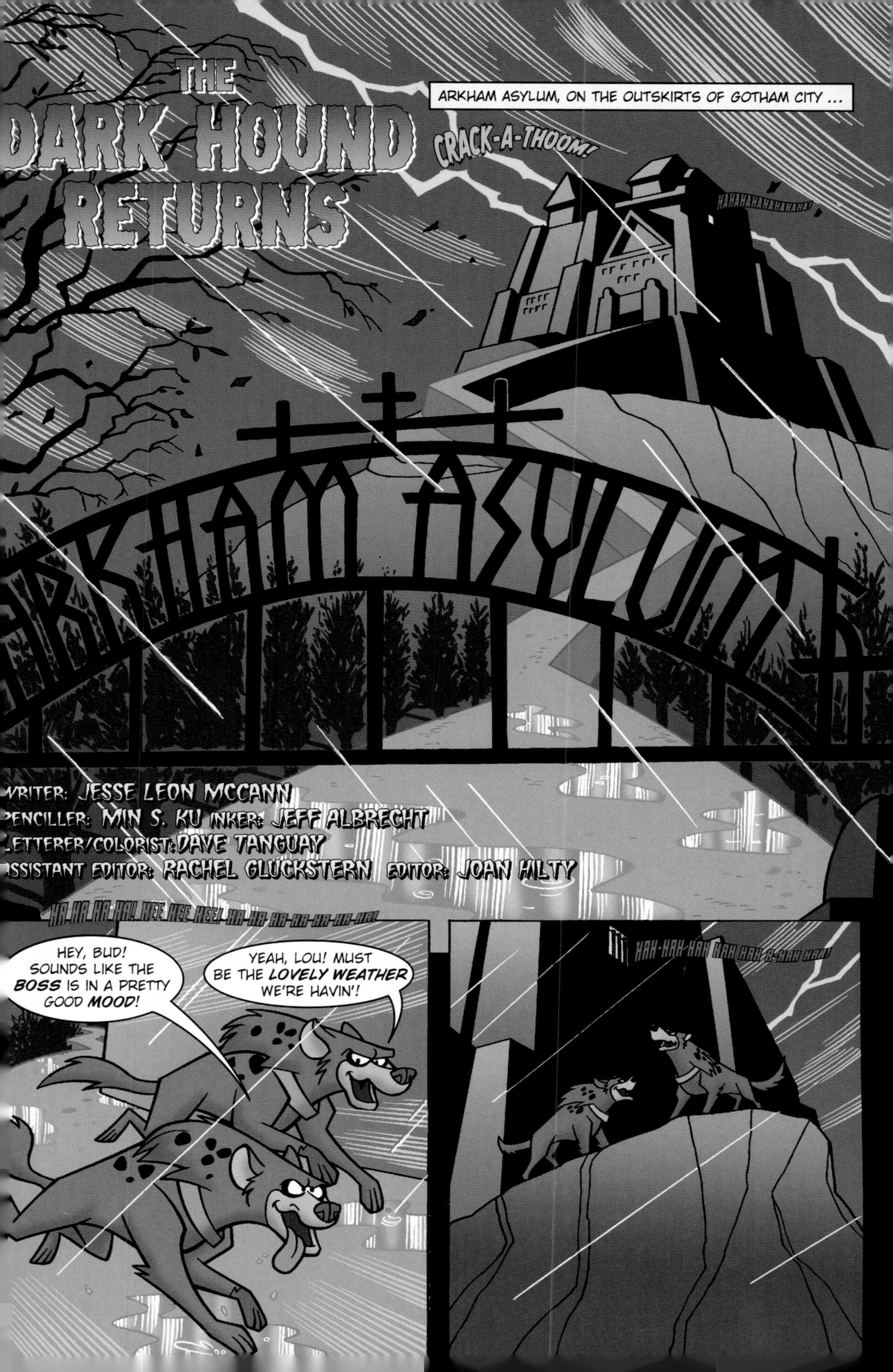
THE DARK HOUND RETURNS
ARKHAM ASYLUM, ON THE OUTSKIRTS OF GOTHAM CITY ...
CRACK-A-THOOM!
HAHAHAHAHAHAHAHA!
ARKHAM ASYLUM
WRITER: JESSE LEON MCCANN
PENCILLER: MIN S. KU INKER: JEFF ALBRECHT
LETTERER/COLORIST: DAVE TANGUAY
ASSISTANT EDITOR: RACHEL GLUCKSTERN EDITOR: JOAN HILTY
HA-HA-HA-HA! HEE HEE HEE! HA-HA HA-HA-HA-HA-HA!
HEY, BUD! SOUNDS LIKE THE BOSS IS IN A PRETTY GOOD MOOD!
YEAH, LOU! MUST BE THE LOVELY WEATHER WE'RE HAVIN'!
HAH-HAH-HAH HAH HAH HAH-A-HAH HAH!

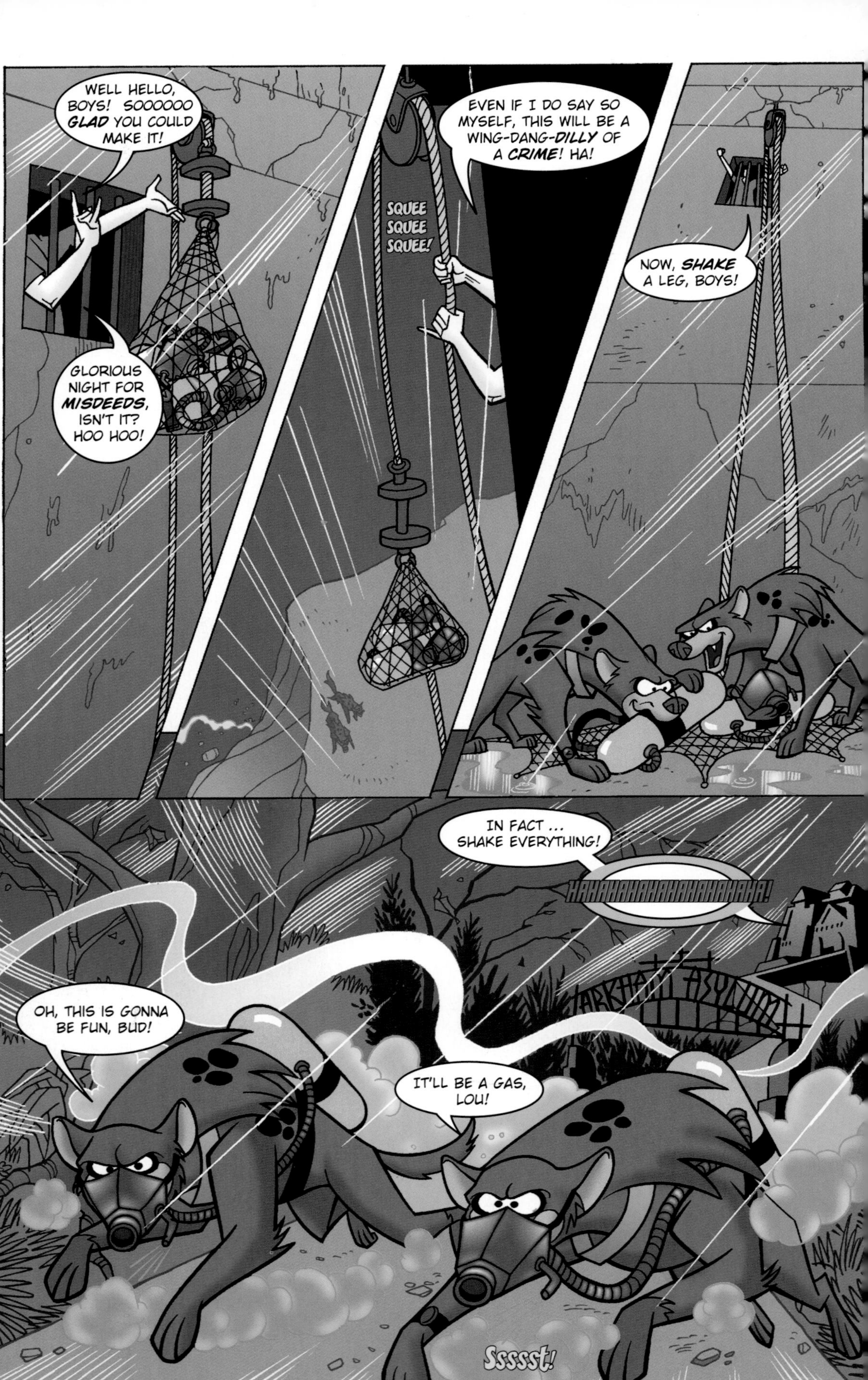
WELL HELLO, BOYS! SOOOOOO GLAD YOU COULD MAKE IT!
GLORIOUS NIGHT FOR MISDEEDS, ISN'T IT? HOO HOO!
EVEN IF I DO SAY SO MYSELF, THIS WILL BE A WING-DANG-DILLY OF A CRIME! HA!
SQUEE SQUEE SQUEE!
NOW, SHAKE A LEG, BOYS!
IN FACT ... SHAKE EVERYTHING!
HAHAHAHAHAHAHAHAHAHA!
ARKHAM ASYLUM
OH, THIS IS GONNA BE FUN, BUD!
IT'LL BE A GAS, LOU!
Ssssst!

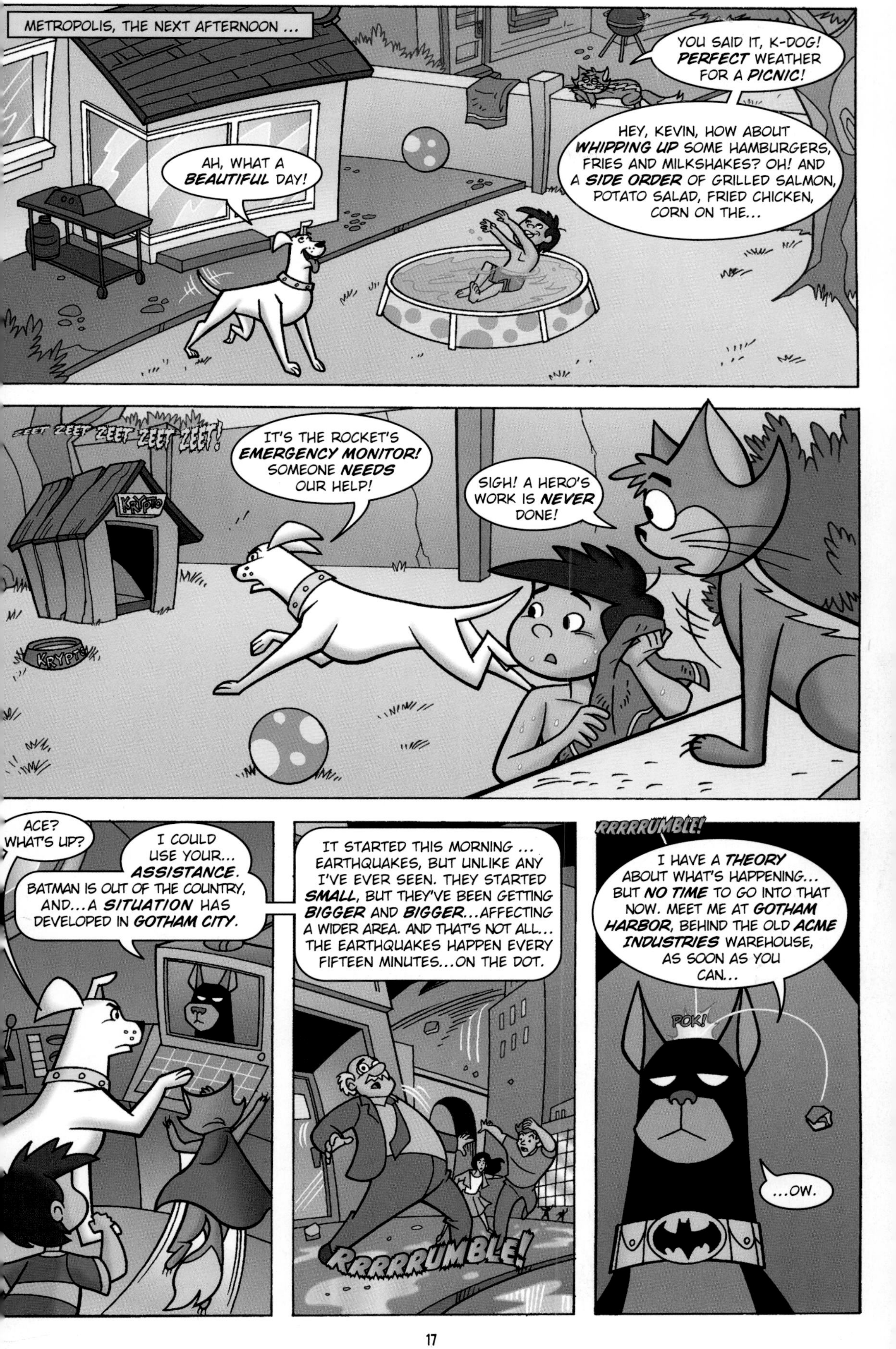
METROPOLIS, THE NEXT AFTERNOON ...
AH, WHAT A BEAUTIFUL DAY!
YOU SAID IT, K-DOG! PERFECT WEATHER FOR A PICNIC!
HEY, KEVIN, HOW ABOUT WHIPPING UP SOME HAMBURGERS, FRIES AND MILKSHAKES? OH! AND A SIDE ORDER OF GRILLED SALMON, POTATO SALAD, FRIED CHICKEN, CORN ON THE...
ZEET ZEET ZEET ZEET ZEET!
KRYPTO
KRYPTO
IT'S THE ROCKET'S EMERGENCY MONITOR! SOMEONE NEEDS OUR HELP!
SIGH! A HERO'S WORK IS NEVER DONE!
ACE? WHAT'S UP?
I COULD USE YOUR... ASSISTANCE. BATMAN IS OUT OF THE COUNTRY, AND...A SITUATION HAS DEVELOPED IN GOTHAM CITY.
IT STARTED THIS MORNING ... EARTHQUAKES, BUT UNLIKE ANY I'VE EVER SEEN. THEY STARTED SMALL, BUT THEY'VE BEEN GETTING BIGGER AND BIGGER...AFFECTING A WIDER AREA. AND THAT'S NOT ALL... THE EARTHQUAKES HAPPEN EVERY FIFTEEN MINUTES...ON THE DOT.
RRRRRUMBLE!
RRRRRUMBLE!
I HAVE A THEORY ABOUT WHAT'S HAPPENING... BUT NO TIME TO GO INTO THAT NOW. MEET ME AT GOTHAM HARBOR, BEHIND THE OLD ACME INDUSTRIES WAREHOUSE, AS SOON AS YOU CAN...
POK!
...OW.

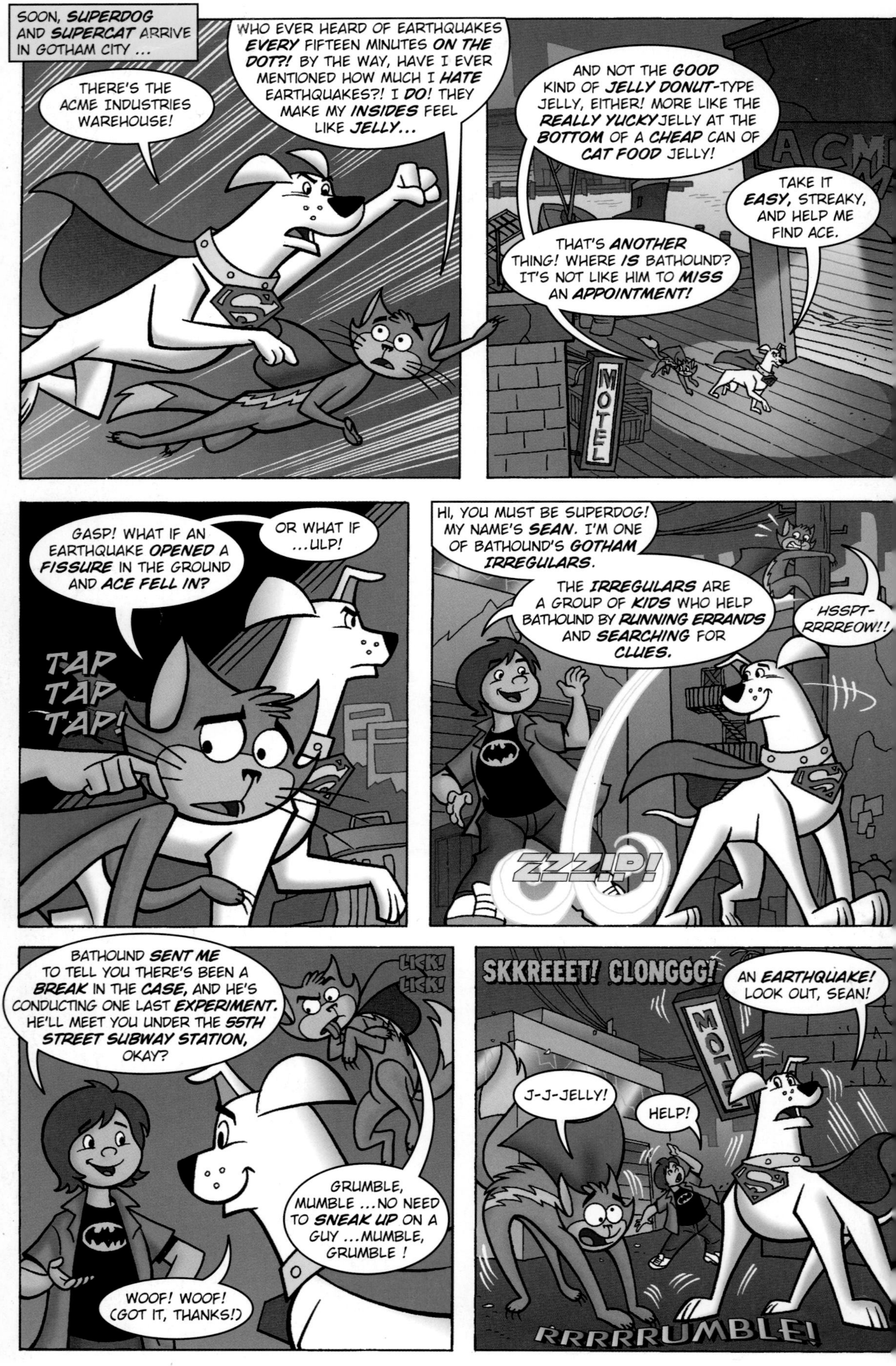
SOON, SUPERDOG AND SUPERCAT ARRIVE IN GOTHAM CITY ...
THERE'S THE ACME INDUSTRIES WAREHOUSE!
WHO EVER HEARD OF EARTHQUAKES EVERY FIFTEEN MINUTES ON THE DOT?! BY THE WAY, HAVE I EVER MENTIONED HOW MUCH I HATE EARTHQUAKES?! I DO! THEY MAKE MY INSIDES FEEL LIKE JELLY...
AND NOT THE GOOD KIND OF JELLY DONUT-TYPE JELLY, EITHER! MORE LIKE THE REALLY YUCKY JELLY AT THE BOTTOM OF A CHEAP CAN OF CAT FOOD JELLY!
TAKE IT EASY, STREAKY, AND HELP ME FIND ACE.
THAT'S ANOTHER THING! WHERE IS BATHOUND? IT'S NOT LIKE HIM TO MISS AN APPOINTMENT!
MOTEL
GASP! WHAT IF AN EARTHQUAKE OPENED A FISSURE IN THE GROUND AND ACE FELL IN?
OR WHAT IF ...ULP!
TAP TAP TAP!
HI, YOU MUST BE SUPERDOG! MY NAME'S SEAN. I'M ONE OF BATHOUND'S GOTHAM IRREGULARS.
THE IRREGULARS ARE A GROUP OF KIDS WHO HELP BATHOUND BY RUNNING ERRANDS AND SEARCHING FOR CLUES.
HSSPT-RRRREOW!!
ZZZIP!
BATHOUND SENT ME TO TELL YOU THERE'S BEEN A BREAK IN THE CASE, AND HE'S CONDUCTING ONE LAST EXPERIMENT. HE'LL MEET YOU UNDER THE 55TH STREET SUBWAY STATION, OKAY?
LICK! LICK!
GRUMBLE, MUMBLE ...NO NEED TO SNEAK UP ON A GUY ...MUMBLE, GRUMBLE !
WOOF! WOOF! (GOT IT, THANKS!)
SKKREEET! CLONGGG!
AN EARTHQUAKE! LOOK OUT, SEAN!
J-J-JELLY!
HELP!
RRRRRUMBLE!

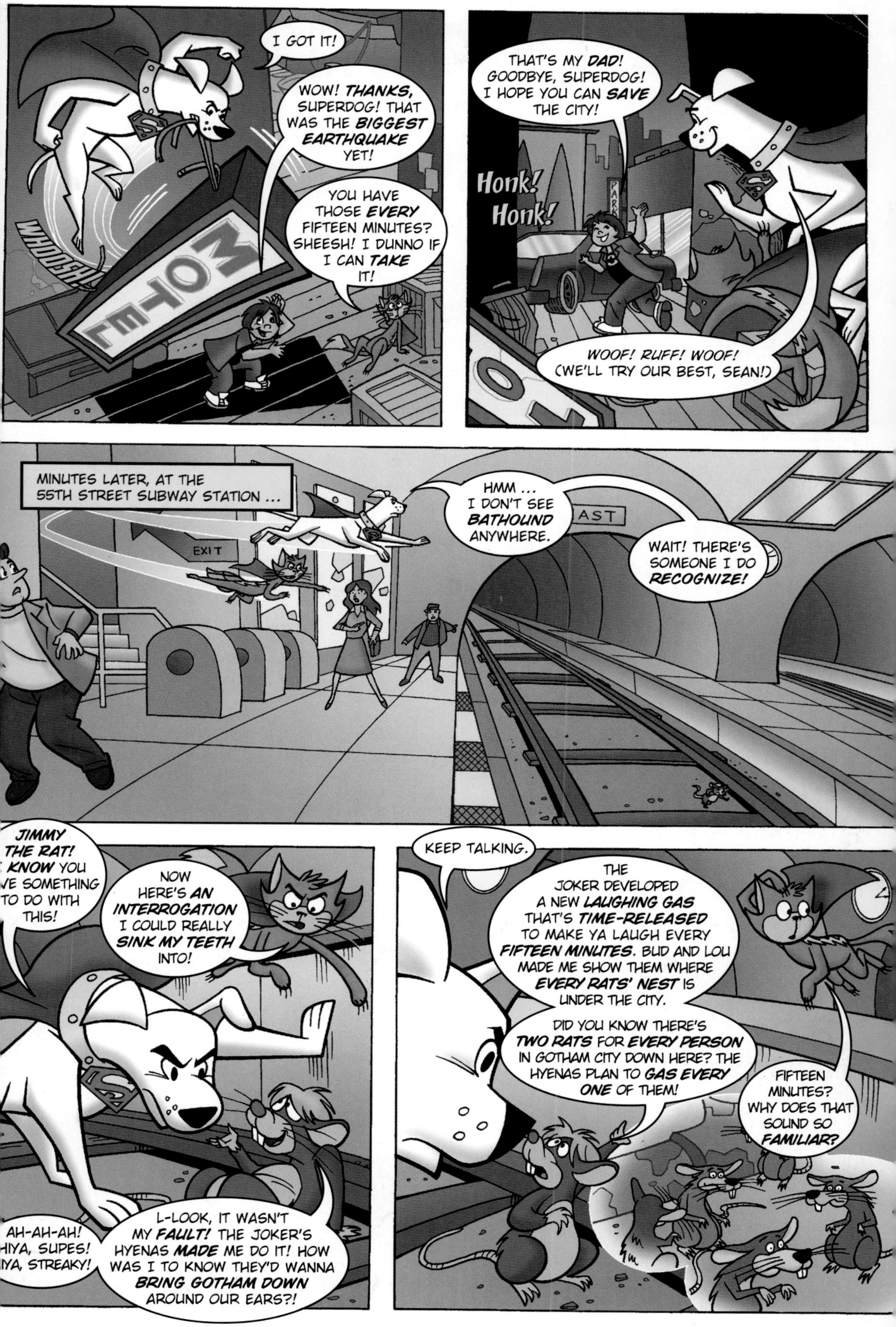

I GOT IT!
WOW! THANKS, SUPERDOG! THAT WAS THE BIGGEST EARTHQUAKE YET!
YOU HAVE THOSE EVERY FIFTEEN MINUTES? SHEESH! I DUNNO IF I CAN TAKE IT!
WHOOSH!
MOTEL
THAT'S MY DAD! GOODBYE, SUPERDOG! I HOPE YOU CAN SAVE THE CITY!
Honk! Honk!
WOOF! RUFF! WOOF! (WE'LL TRY OUR BEST, SEAN!)
MINUTES LATER, AT THE 55TH STREET SUBWAY STATION ...
HMM ... I DON'T SEE BATHOUND ANYWHERE.
WAIT! THERE'S SOMEONE I DO RECOGNIZE!
EXIT
AST
JIMMY THE RAT! KNOW YOU VE SOMETHING TO DO WITH THIS!
NOW HERE'S AN INTERROGATION I COULD REALLY SINK MY TEETH INTO!
AH-AH-AH! HIYA, SUPES! IYA, STREAKY!
L-LOOK, IT WASN'T MY FAULT! THE JOKER'S HYENAS MADE ME DO IT! HOW WAS I TO KNOW THEY'D WANNA BRING GOTHAM DOWN AROUND OUR EARS?!
KEEP TALKING.
THE JOKER DEVELOPED A NEW LAUGHING GAS THAT'S TIME-RELEASED TO MAKE YA LAUGH EVERY FIFTEEN MINUTES. BUD AND LOU MADE ME SHOW THEM WHERE EVERY RATS' NEST IS UNDER THE CITY.
DID YOU KNOW THERE'S TWO RATS FOR EVERY PERSON IN GOTHAM CITY DOWN HERE? THE HYENAS PLAN TO GAS EVERY ONE OF THEM!
FIFTEEN MINUTES? WHY DOES THAT SOUND SO FAMILIAR?

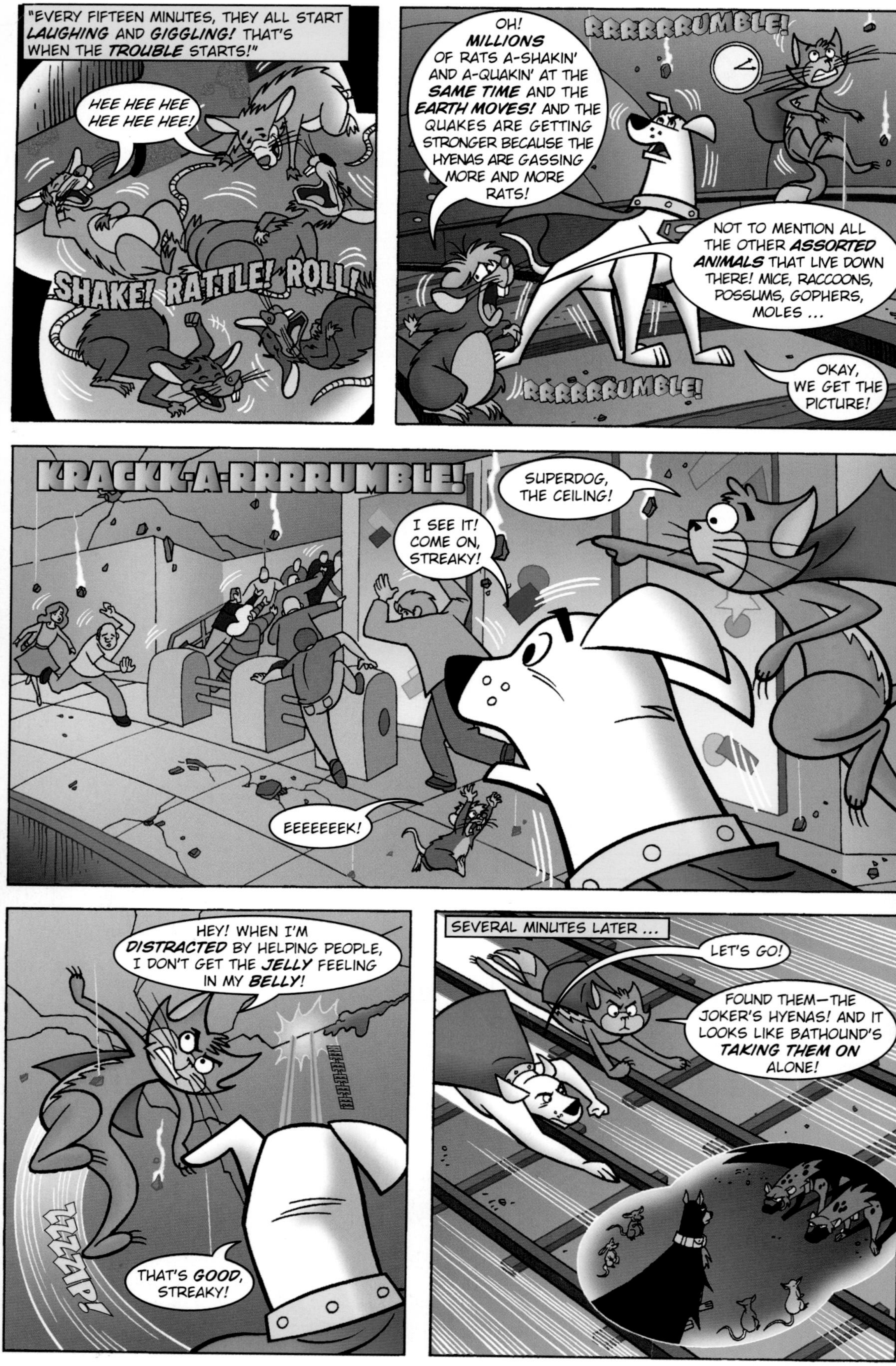
"EVERY FIFTEEN MINUTES, THEY ALL START LAUGHING AND GIGGLING! THAT'S WHEN THE TROUBLE STARTS!"
HEE HEE HEE HEE HEE HEE!
SHAKE! RATTLE! ROLL!
OH! MILLIONS OF RATS A-SHAKIN' AND A-QUAKIN' AT THE SAME TIME AND THE EARTH MOVES! AND THE QUAKES ARE GETTING STRONGER BECAUSE THE HYENAS ARE GASSING MORE AND MORE RATS!
RRRRRRUMBLE!
NOT TO MENTION ALL THE OTHER ASSORTED ANIMALS THAT LIVE DOWN THERE! MICE, RACCOONS, POSSUMS, GOPHERS, MOLES ...
RRRRRRUMBLE!
OKAY, WE GET THE PICTURE!
KRACKK-A-RRRRUMBLE!
SUPERDOG, THE CEILING!
I SEE IT! COME ON, STREAKY!
EEEEEEEK!
HEY! WHEN I'M DISTRACTED BY HELPING PEOPLE, I DON'T GET THE JELLY FEELING IN MY BELLY!
ZZZZIP!
THAT'S GOOD, STREAKY!
SEVERAL MINUTES LATER ...
LET'S GO!
FOUND THEM—THE JOKER'S HYENAS! AND IT LOOKS LIKE BATHOUND'S TAKING THEM ON ALONE!

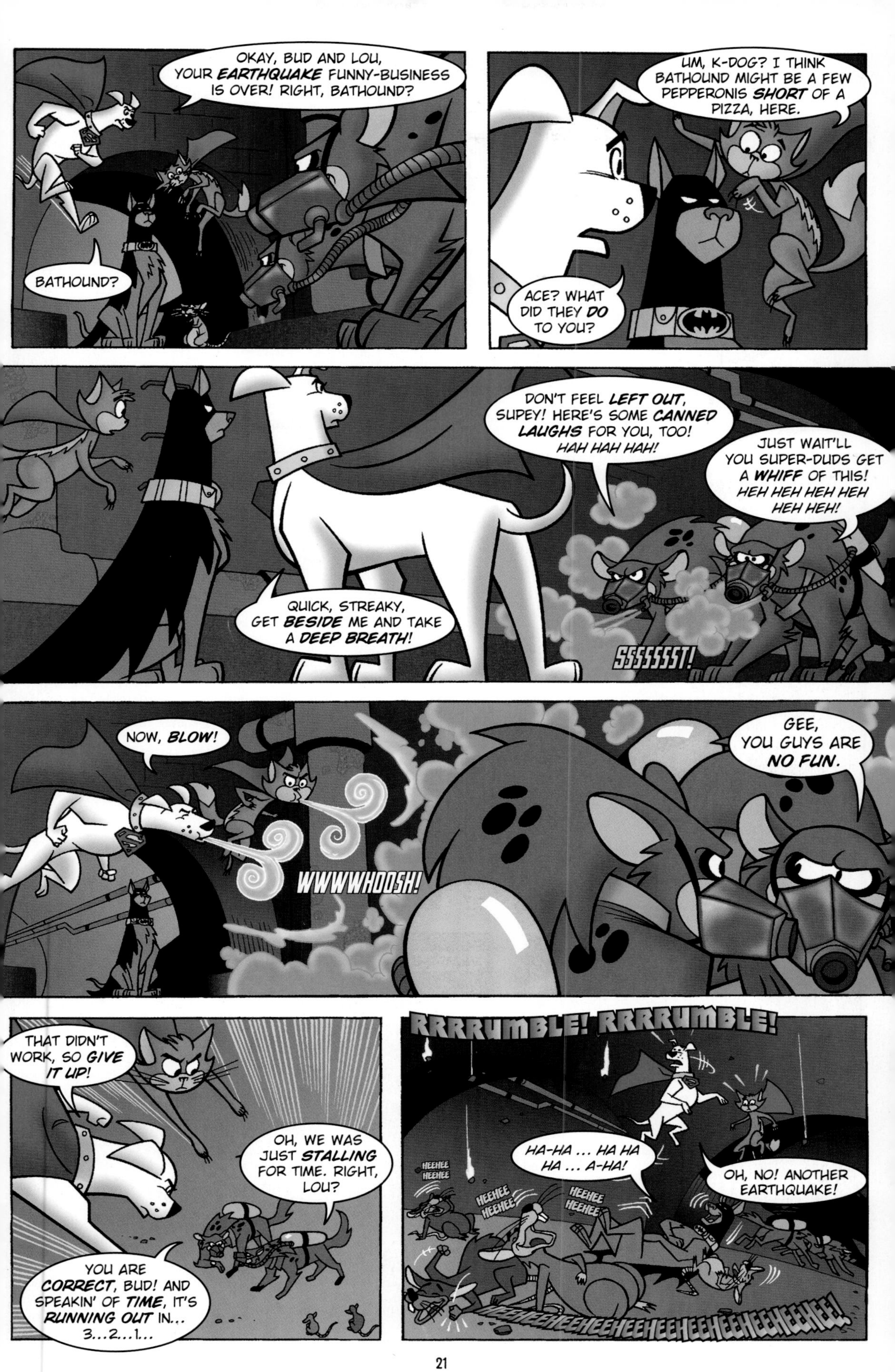
OKAY, BUD AND LOU, YOUR EARTHQUAKE FUNNY-BUSINESS IS OVER! RIGHT, BATHOUND?
BATHOUND?
UM, K-DOG? I THINK BATHOUND MIGHT BE A FEW PEPPERONIS SHORT OF A PIZZA, HERE.
ACE? WHAT DID THEY DO TO YOU?
DON'T FEEL LEFT OUT, SUPEY! HERE'S SOME CANNED LAUGHS FOR YOU, TOO! HAH HAH HAH!
JUST WAIT'LL YOU SUPER-DUDS GET A WHIFF OF THIS! HEH HEH HEH HEH HEH HEH!
QUICK, STREAKY, GET BESIDE ME AND TAKE A DEEP BREATH!
SSSSSSST!
NOW, BLOW!
GEE, YOU GUYS ARE NO FUN.
WWWWHOOSH!
THAT DIDN'T WORK, SO GIVE IT UP!
OH, WE WAS JUST STALLING FOR TIME. RIGHT, LOU?
YOU ARE CORRECT, BUD! AND SPEAKIN' OF TIME, IT'S RUNNING OUT IN... 3...2...1...
RRRRUMBLE! RRRRUMBLE!
HA-HA ... HA HA HA ... A-HA!
OH, NO! ANOTHER EARTHQUAKE!
HEEHEE HEEHEE
HEEHEE HEEHEE
HEEHEE HEEHEE
HEEHEEHEEHEEHEEHEEHEEHEEHEEHEEHEEHEEHEEHEE!

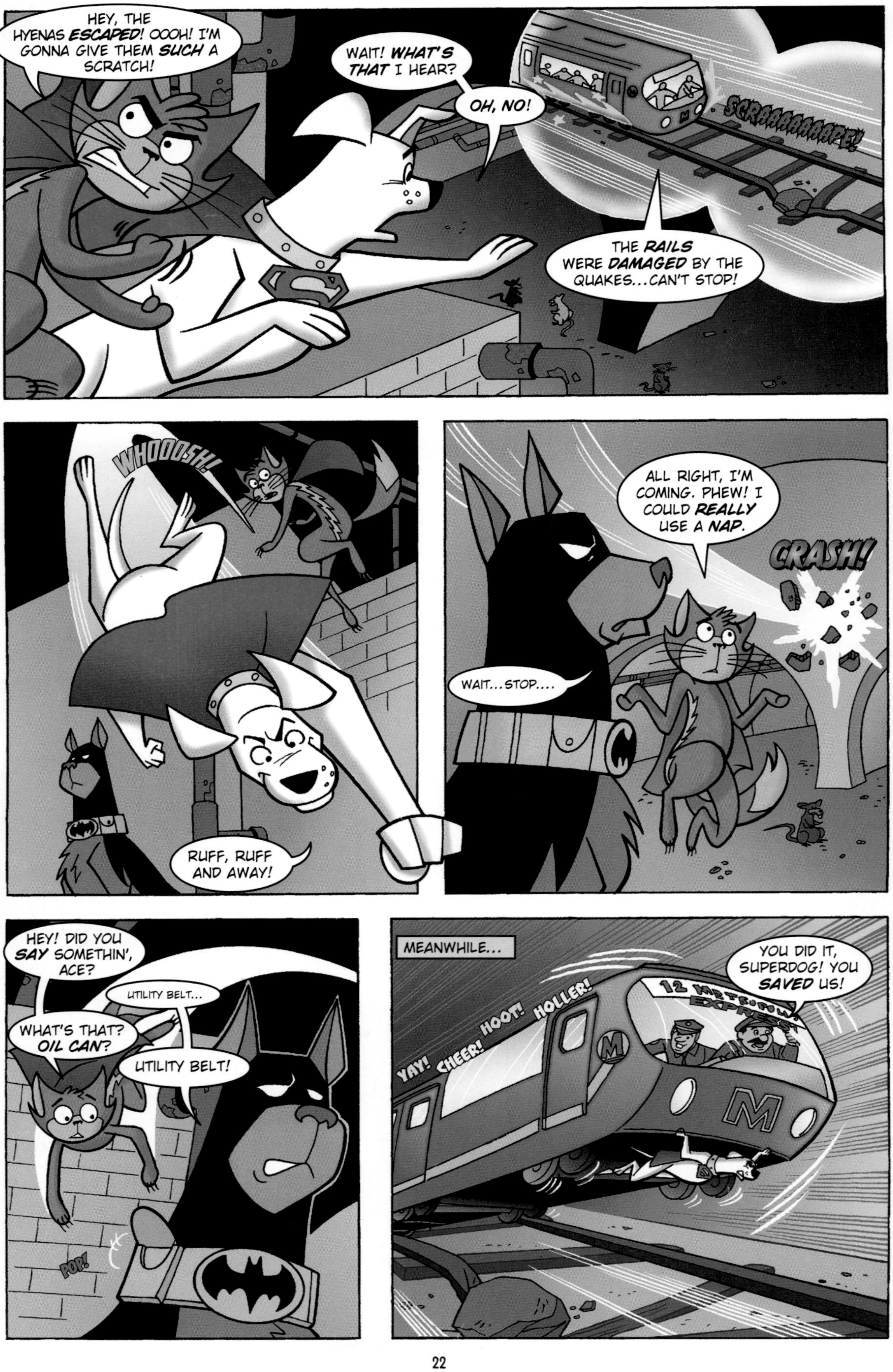
HEY, THE HYENAS ESCAPED! OOOH! I'M GONNA GIVE THEM SUCH A SCRATCH!
WAIT! WHAT'S THAT I HEAR?
OH, NO!
SCRAAAAAAAAPE!
THE RAILS WERE DAMAGED BY THE QUAKES...CAN'T STOP!
WHOOOSH!
RUFF, RUFF AND AWAY!
ALL RIGHT, I'M COMING. PHEW! I COULD REALLY USE A NAP.
CRASH!
WAIT...STOP....
HEY! DID YOU SAY SOMETHIN', ACE?
UTILITY BELT...
WHAT'S THAT? OIL CAN?
UTILITY BELT!
POP!
MEANWHILE...
YOU DID IT, SUPERDOG! YOU SAVED US!
YAY! CHEER! HOOT! HOLLER!

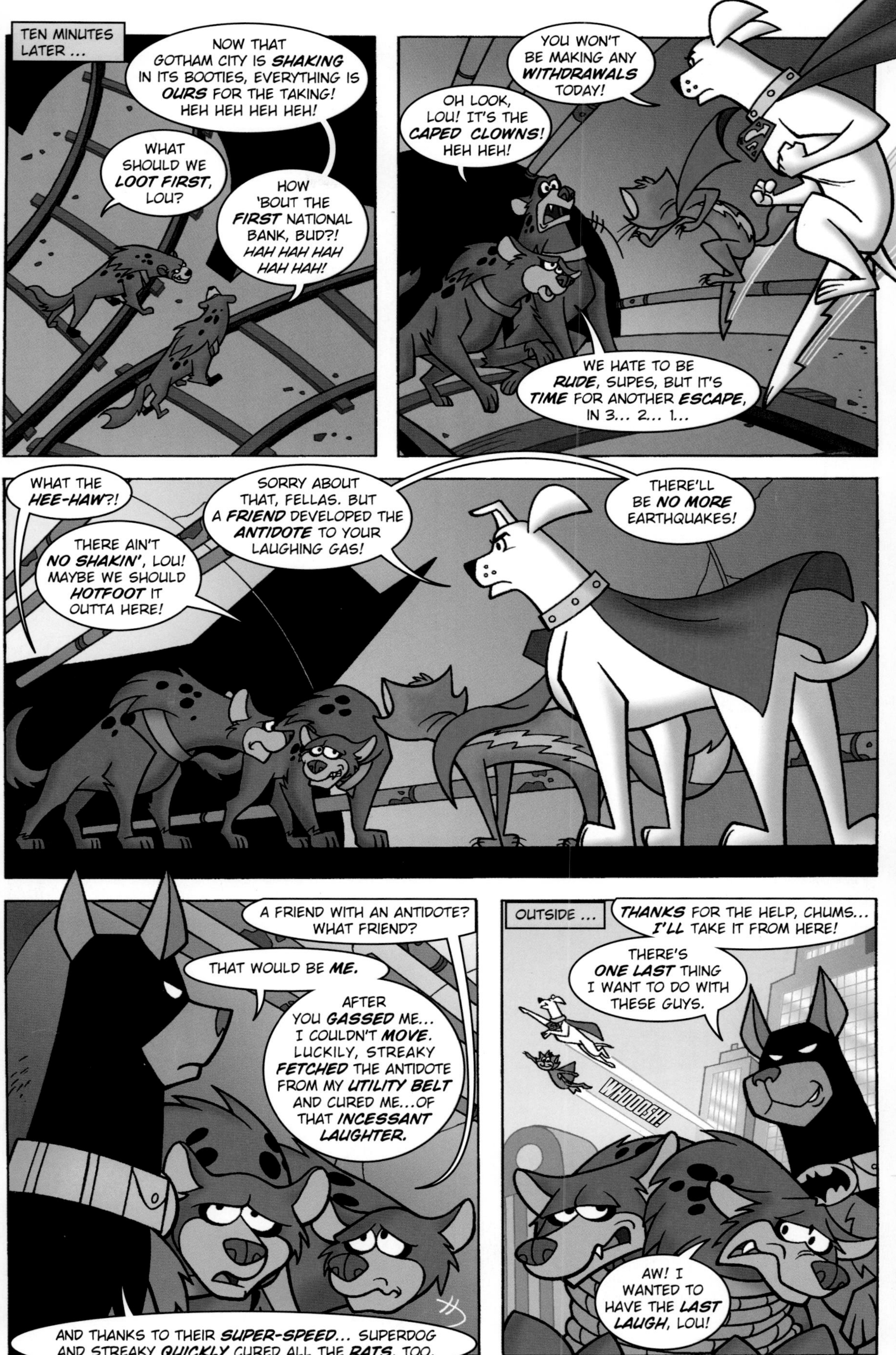
TEN MINUTES LATER ...
NOW THAT GOTHAM CITY IS SHAKING IN ITS BOOTIES, EVERYTHING IS OURS FOR THE TAKING! HEH HEH HEH HEH!
WHAT SHOULD WE LOOT FIRST, LOU?
HOW 'BOUT THE FIRST NATIONAL BANK, BUD?! HAH HAH HAH HAH HAH!
YOU WON'T BE MAKING ANY WITHDRAWALS TODAY!
OH LOOK, LOU! IT'S THE CAPED CLOWNS! HEH HEH!
WE HATE TO BE RUDE, SUPES, BUT IT'S TIME FOR ANOTHER ESCAPE, IN 3... 2... 1...
WHAT THE HEE-HAW?!
THERE AIN'T NO SHAKIN', LOU! MAYBE WE SHOULD HOTFOOT IT OUTTA HERE!
SORRY ABOUT THAT, FELLAS. BUT A FRIEND DEVELOPED THE ANTIDOTE TO YOUR LAUGHING GAS!
THERE'LL BE NO MORE EARTHQUAKES!
A FRIEND WITH AN ANTIDOTE? WHAT FRIEND?
THAT WOULD BE ME.
AFTER YOU GASSED ME... I COULDN'T MOVE. LUCKILY, STREAKY FETCHED THE ANTIDOTE FROM MY UTILITY BELT AND CURED ME...OF THAT INCESSANT LAUGHTER.
AND THANKS TO THEIR SUPER-SPEED... SUPERDOG AND STREAKY QUICKLY CURED ALL THE RATS, TOO.
OUTSIDE ...
THANKS FOR THE HELP, CHUMS... I'LL TAKE IT FROM HERE!
THERE'S ONE LAST THING I WANT TO DO WITH THESE GUYS.
WHOOOSH!
AW! I WANTED TO HAVE THE LAST LAUGH, LOU!

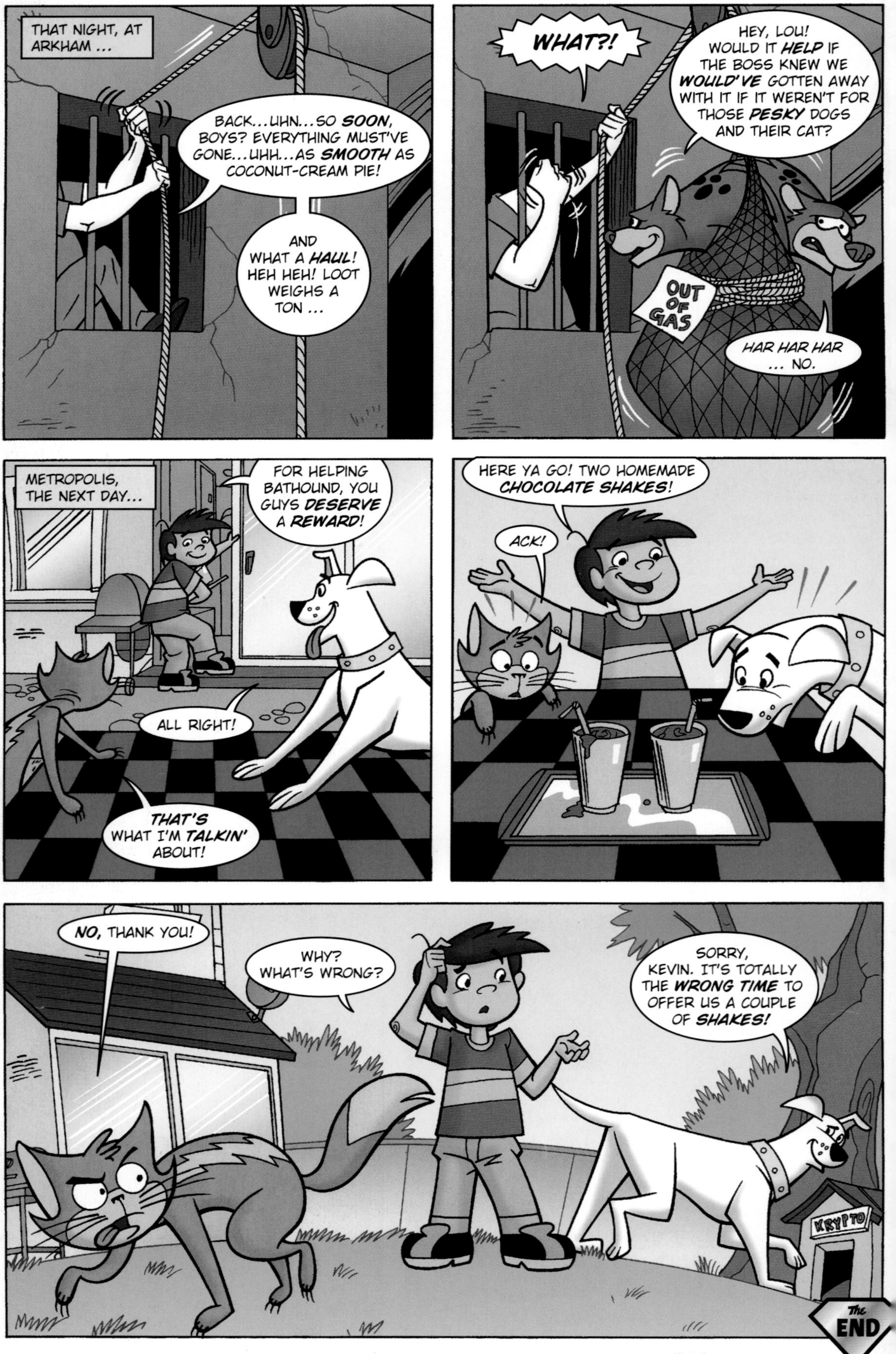
THAT NIGHT, AT ARKHAM ...
BACK...UHN...SO SOON, BOYS? EVERYTHING MUST'VE GONE...UHH...AS SMOOTH AS COCONUT-CREAM PIE!
AND WHAT A HAUL! HEH HEH! LOOT WEIGHS A TON ...
WHAT?!
HEY, LOU! WOULD IT HELP IF THE BOSS KNEW WE WOULD'VE GOTTEN AWAY WITH IT IF IT WEREN'T FOR THOSE PESKY DOGS AND THEIR CAT?
OUT OF GAS
HAR HAR HAR ... NO.
METROPOLIS, THE NEXT DAY...
FOR HELPING BATHOUND, YOU GUYS DESERVE A REWARD!
ALL RIGHT!
THAT'S WHAT I'M TALKIN' ABOUT!
HERE YA GO! TWO HOMEMADE CHOCOLATE SHAKES!
ACK!
NO, THANK YOU!
WHY? WHAT'S WRONG?
SORRY, KEVIN. IT'S TOTALLY THE WRONG TIME TO OFFER US A COUPLE OF SHAKES!
KRYPTO
The END

Superdog Jokes!

WHAT KIND OF DOG TELLS THE TIME?

A WATCH DOG!

WHAT DO YOU CALL A SUPERDOG WEARING METAL ARMOR?

KRYPTO-KNIGHT!

WHY IS A TREE LIKE A BIG DOG?

THEY BOTH HAVE A LOT OF BARK!

WHAT DO YOU CALL A DOG THAT MUMBLES?

A MUTT-ERER!

Creators

JESSE LEON MCCANN WRITER

Jesse Leon McCann is a *New York Times* Top-Ten Children's Book Writer, as well as a prolific all-ages comics writer. His credits include Pinky and the Brain, Animaniacs, and Looney Tunes for DC Comics; Scooby-Doo and Shrek 2 for Scholastic; and The Simpsons and Futurama for Bongo Comics. He lives in Los Angeles with his wife and four cats.

MIN SUNG KU PENCILLER

As a young child, Min Sung Ku dreamed of becoming a comic book illustrator. At six years old, he drew a picture of Superman standing behind the American flag. He has since achieved his childhood dream, having illustrated popular licensed comics properties like the Justice League, Batman Beyond, Spider-Man, Ben 10, Phineas & Ferb, the Replacements, the Proud Family, Krpyto the Superdog, and, of course, Superman. Min lives with his lovely wife and their beautiful twin daughters, Elisia and Eliana.

DAVE TANGUAY COLORIST/LETTERER

David Tanguay has over 20 years of experience in the comic book industry. He has worked as an editor, layout artist, colorist, and letterer. He has also done web design, and he taught computer graphics at the State University of New York.

Glossary

GOTHAM CITY (GAH-thum SIT-ee) – Batman and Ace the Bathound's home city

INTERROGATION (in-tare-uh-GAY-shuhn) – the process of questioning someone in detail, often in order to determine if someone is guilty or innocent of a crime

KRYPTON (KRIP-tahn) – Superman and Krypto the Superdog's home planet

METROPOLIS (meh-TROHP-uhl-uhss) – Superman and Krypto the Superdog's adopted home city

MISDEEDS (miss-DEEDZ) – immoral or evil acts

RECOGNIZE (REK-uhg-nize) – to see someone and know who the person is, or to understand a situation and know it is true or right

UTILITY BELT (yoo-TILL-uh-tee BELT) – Batman and Ace the Bathound both wear Utility Belts that hold all sorts of tools and crime-fighting gadgets

Visual Questions & Prompts

1. WHAT DO YOU THINK THIS OBJECT IS THAT KRYPTO GAVE KEVIN WHEN THEY FIRST MET?

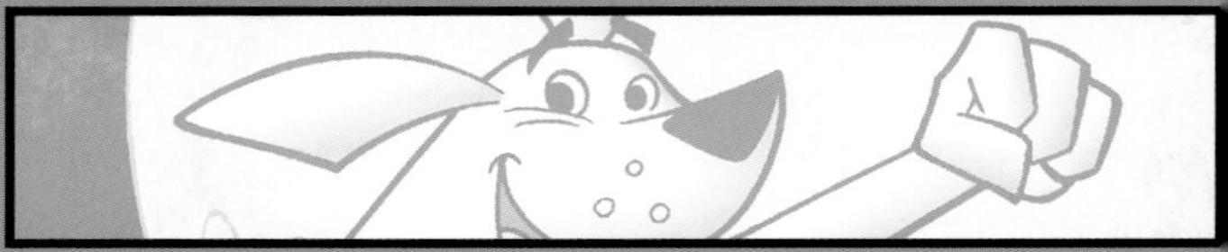

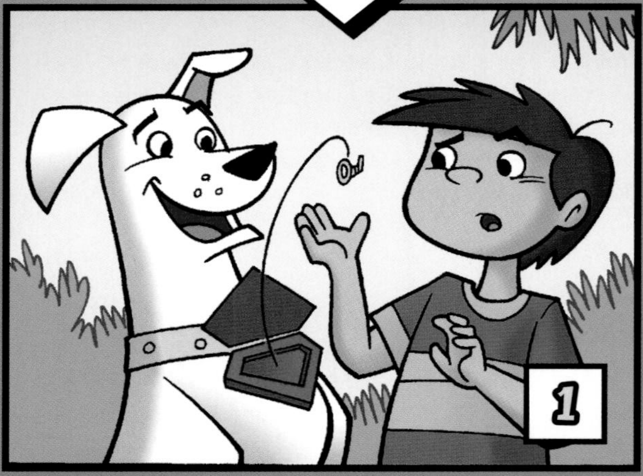
1

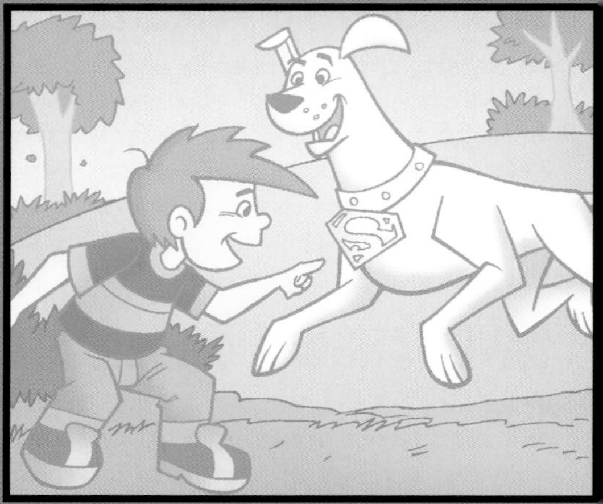

2. WHY DO YOU THINK KRYPTO'S SHIP'S COMPUTER MADE HIM FALL INTO A DEEP SLEEP WHILE HE TRAVELED?

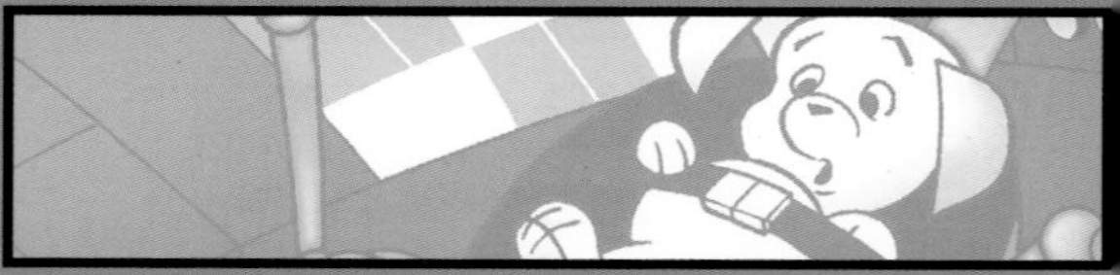

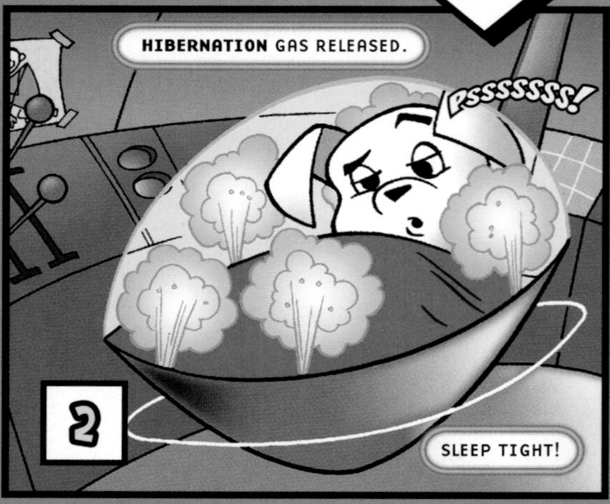
HIBERNATION GAS RELEASED.
PSSSSSSS!
2
SLEEP TIGHT!

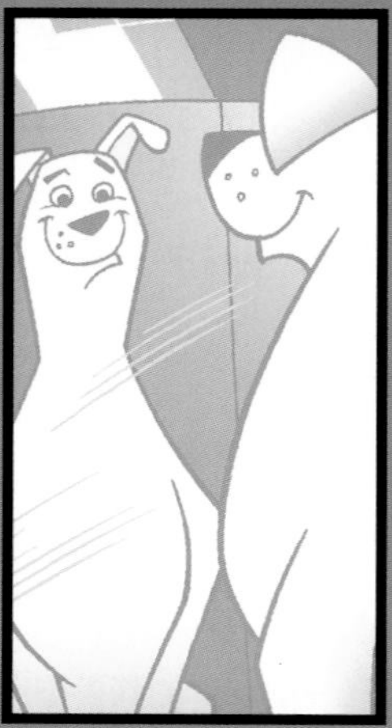

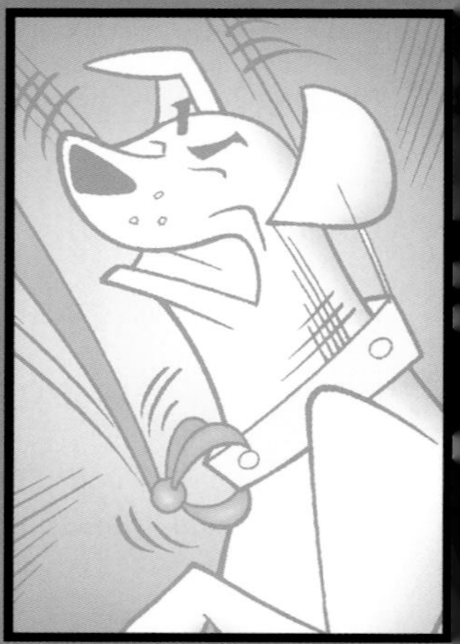

3. WHAT IS HAPPENING IN THIS PANEL? WHAT DOES KRYPTO SEE, AND HOW?

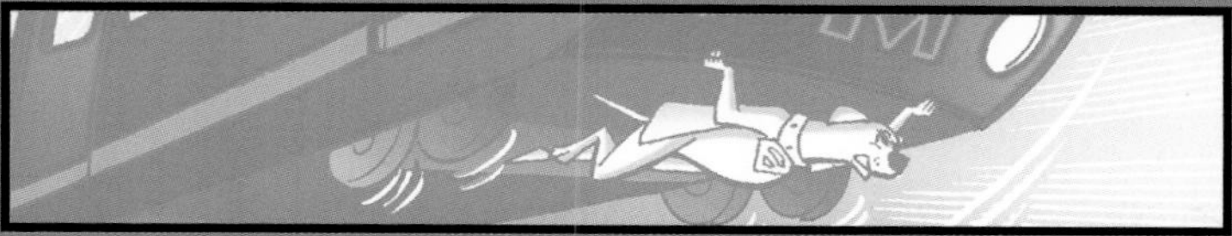

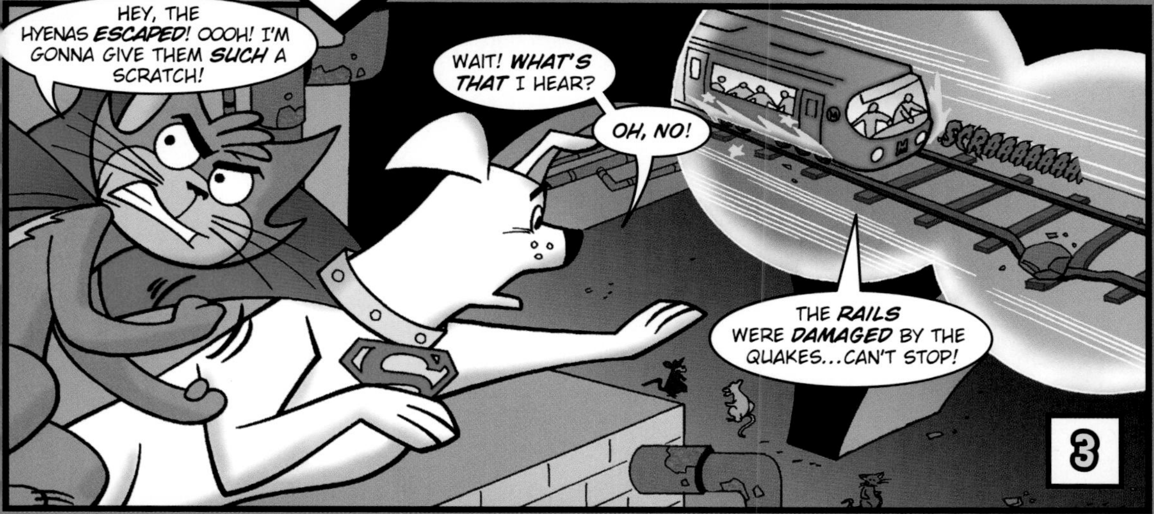
HEY, THE HYENAS *ESCAPED*! OOOH! I'M GONNA GIVE THEM *SUCH* A SCRATCH!
WAIT! *WHAT'S THAT* I HEAR?
OH, NO!
SCRAAAAAAA...
THE *RAILS* WERE *DAMAGED* BY THE QUAKES...CAN'T STOP!
3

4. WHY DON'T SUPERCAT AND SUPERDOG WANT CHOCOLATE MILKSHAKES AT THE END OF THIS BOOK WHEN KEVIN OFFERS TO MAKE SOME?

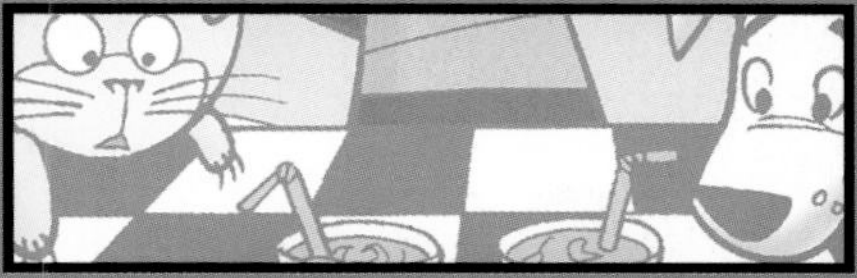

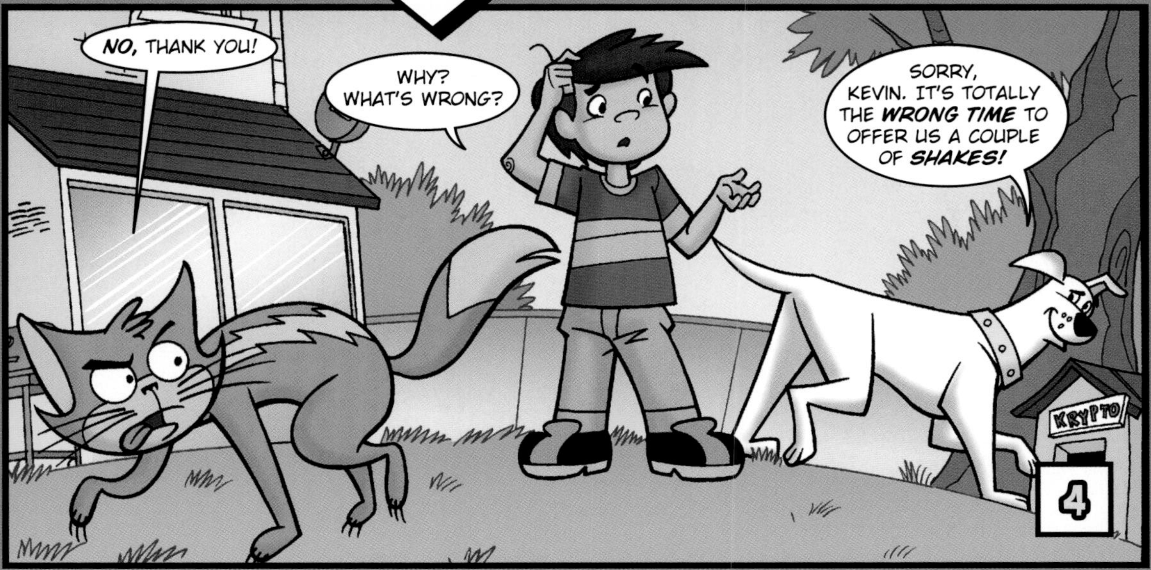
NO, THANK YOU!
WHY? WHAT'S WRONG?
SORRY, KEVIN. IT'S TOTALLY THE *WRONG TIME* TO OFFER US A COUPLE OF *SHAKES!*
KRYPTO
4

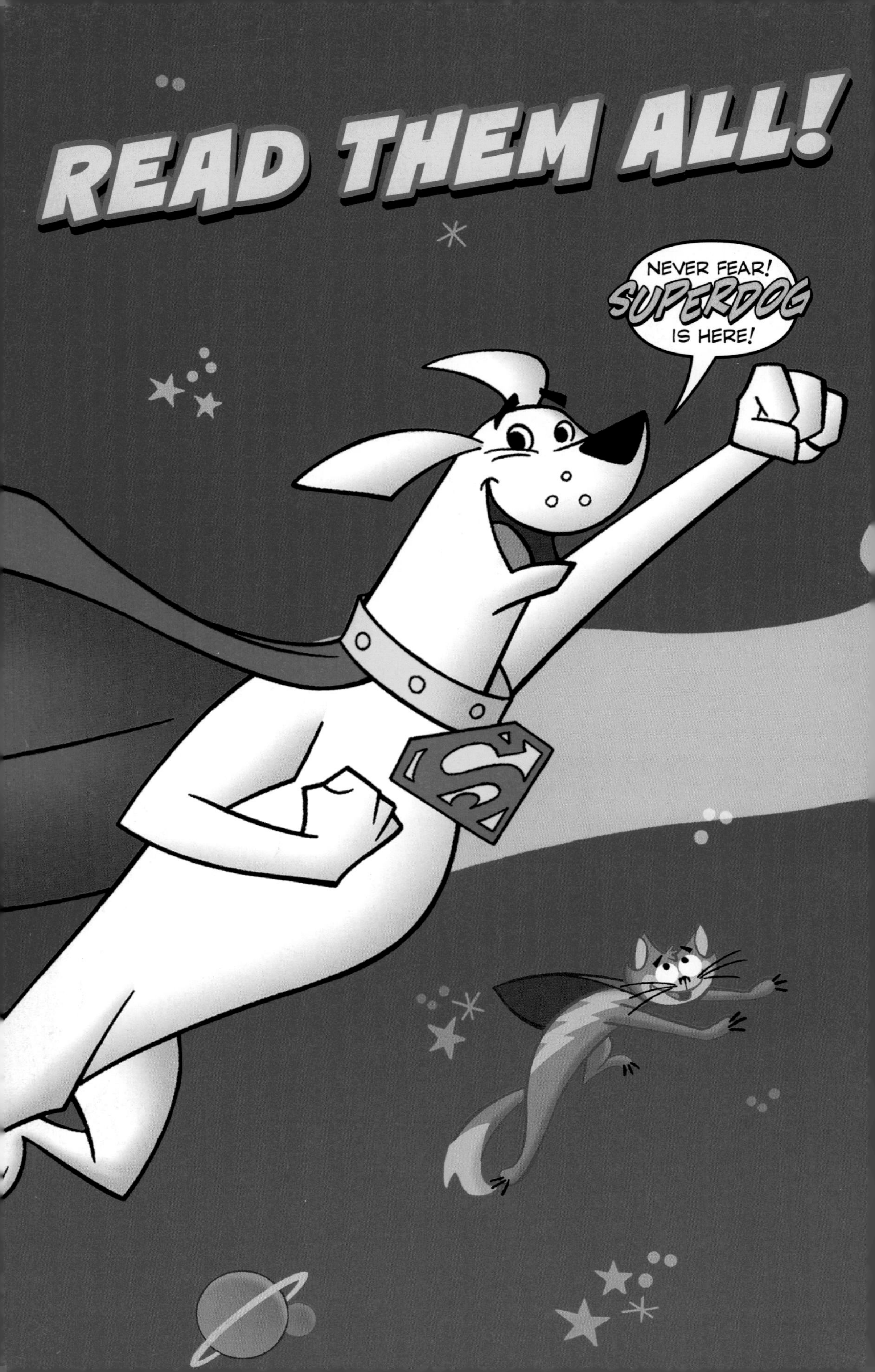
READ THEM ALL!
NEVER FEAR! SUPERDOG IS HERE!

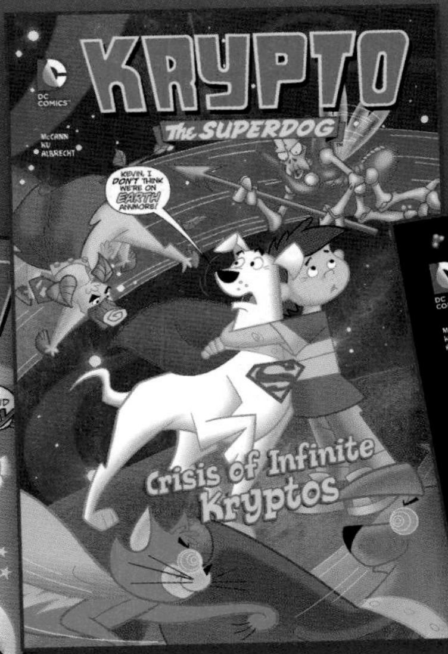
DC COMICS
KRYPTO
The SUPERDOG
McCANN
KU
ALBRECHT
KEVIN, I DON'T THINK WE'RE ON EARTH ANYMORE!
Crisis of Infinite Kryptos

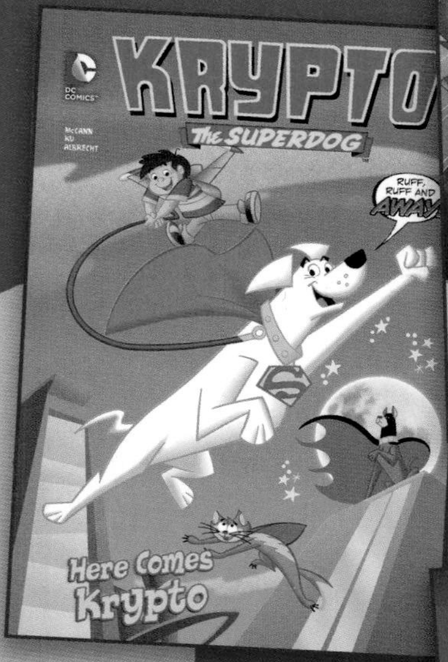
DC COMICS
KRYPTO
The SUPERDOG
McCANN
KU
ALBRECHT
RUFF, RUFF AND AWAY!
Here Comes Krypto

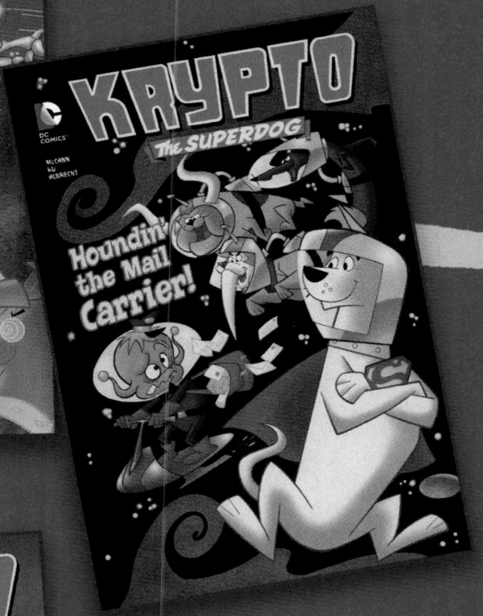
DC COMICS
KRYPTO
The SUPERDOG
McCANN
KU
ALBRECHT
Houndin' the Mail Carrier!

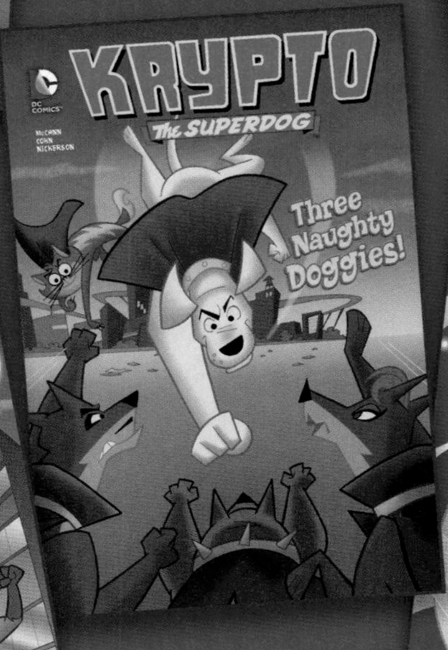
DC COMICS
KRYPTO
The SUPERDOG
McCANN
COHN
NICKERSON
Three Naughty Doggies!

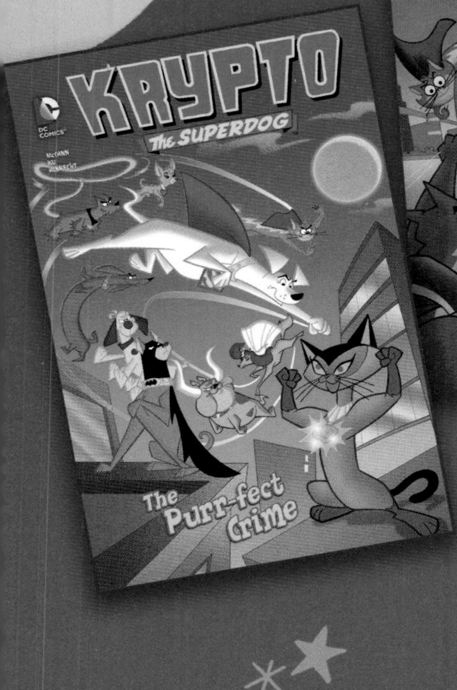
DC COMICS
KRYPTO
The SUPERDOG
McCANN
KU
ALBRECHT
The Purr-fect Crime

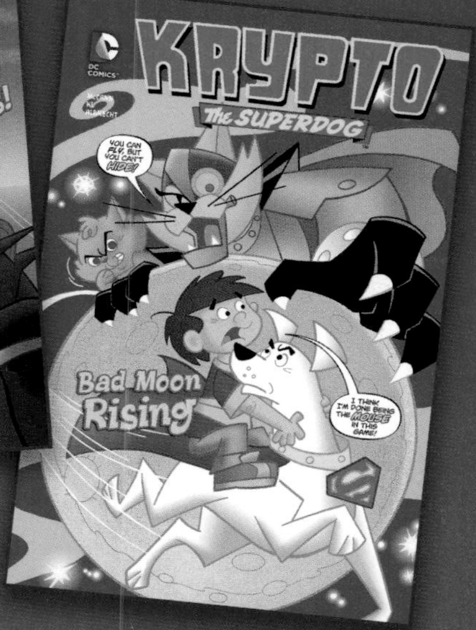
DC COMICS
KRYPTO
The SUPERDOG
McCANN
KU
ALBRECHT
YOU CAN FLY, BUT YOU CAN'T HIDE!
I THINK I'M DONE BEING THE MOUSE IN THIS GAME!
Bad Moon Rising

only from...

STONE ARCH BOOKS™

KRYPTO

The SUPERDOG™

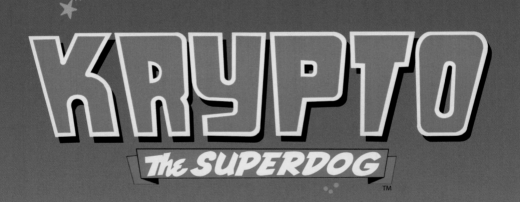